Meghan's Story

Brides of Fall River

CHLOE EMILE

This is a work of fiction. Names, characters, organizations,places, events, and incidents are either products of the author's imagination or are used fictitiously.

Meghan's Story
Copyright © 2015 by Chloe Emile. All rights reserved.

ISBN-13: 978-1987859171
ISBN-10: 1987859170

CONTENTS

CHAPTER ONE

1868, Fall River, Massachusetts

When Meghan came into this world, she was destined to reach the stars. She was the first child born to Abby and Ryan Lochlan. Ten minutes later, a second child, Molly, followed. Not long after that, the third girl, Annie, joined the family.

The triplets all shared the same birthday, but each girl was different, not only in looks but also in personality and temperament.

By the time she was able to walk, raven-haired Meghan positioned herself to be the natural leader of the group. Even though a few years later, their twin brothers Tom and Daniel joined the clan and their cousin Holly came to live with them, Meghan still remained the leader.

At a young age, she developed a great love for books, and her favorite room in the house was the library. Molly, her late grandmother, had been an avid reader and had homeschooled Meghan's mother and aunts.

Although Abby had given Meghan and her siblings the basics in education, they all went to the school in Fall River. Meghan quickly took to the classes, and she was always happy to help her sisters and brothers with their homework problems.

Abby thought maybe Meghan would become a teacher someday, but Meghan had all kinds of talents. Meghan was a tomboy, and she was Ryan's favorite little girl. Her bond with her father was strong, and not even the birth of her twin brothers could detract from it.

Meghan was the first to climb onto a horse without any fear and gallop down the road from the house. While both her sisters preferred to be in the kitchen with their mother, learning how to cook and sew, Meghan was with her dad.

Abby wondered if Meghan would ever grow out of being a tomboy and become a lady like her sisters. She never expected to see the day when that girl would step out of those jeans and flannel shirt and put on a dress. Abby wondered if Meghan would develop an interest in men as she had, when she was her daughter's age.

And then one day it happened.

A young army lieutenant by the name of Michael Tucker rode up to the front door of the house, followed by a few of his men.

To fifteen-year-old Meghan, who was sweeping the top porch, he was the most handsome man she had ever seen. With his dark hair and eyebrows, he was masculine and rugged, like a hero in one of the novels she loved.

He had come to Fall River with a regiment of soldiers to secure the payroll coming by train later that week. A shipment of gold was also being sent to New York by ship the same day. The Secretary himself wanted Michael to turn over the orders to Mr. Lochlan.

He dismounted and came to the door. As he knocked, Meghan scurried inside, tentatively poking her head out the window. A few seconds after, Abby answered the door.

"Hello," she said brightly. "Can I help you, Lieutenant?"

He took off his hat and flashed her his most winsome smile.

"Ma'am, I'm Lieutenant Michael Tucker. I have some orders for a Mr. Ryan Lochlan."

"That would be my husband. Do come in, Lieutenant, and have your men relax." Abby looked out to the men and smiled to welcome them. "Can I get you gentlemen some coffee?"

The lieutenant looked back at the sergeant.

"Sergeant, have the troops dismount."

The sergeant addressed the troops. "Company, dismount."

The troops obeyed. One of them noticed Meghan on the top porch and let out a whistle. Meghan looked away, blushing.

Lieutenant Tucker was quick to set him straight. "Soldier, another outburst like that, and you will go on report." He turned back to Abby. "Ma'am, I apologize for my men."

"Oh, the boy's only giving a compliment to my daughter. Meghan, you get inside and tell your daddy he's got company." She turned back to the lieutenant. "Won't you come inside?" She stepped back to allow him into the house. She pointed in the direction of the library. "Do make yourself at home. My husband should be down directly."

She left him to go to the back end of the house. A few minutes passed before an older gentlemen came in.

Lieutenant Tucker imagined it must be Mr. Lochlan. He stood up. "Mr. Lochlan?"

Ryan nodded amiably. "Yes. My daughter tells me you have some orders for me, Lieutenant?"

Lieutenant Tucker took out an envelope from the inside of his shirt.

"Sir, I was told by the secretary that you would know what to do after you read this." He handed Ryan the envelope.

As Ryan read the contents, the expression on his face turned serious. He looked up at the lieutenant. "Are you aware of what is in this document, Lieutenant?"

"Yes, sir, I am. I have been sent here to make sure these orders are followed out."

Ryan needed a plan. He had to find a way to teach this new lieutenant how things were done out here.

"I would like to suggest that your troops scatter about. It would be a better idea since if stragglers do plan on stealing the gold, they are not going to do it in a group. And they will not take on a regiment of soldiers."

"Yes, sir."

Ryan figured the lieutenant had to be right out of the academy, to snap with the *sirs* so much.

"One more thing, Lieutenant. I'm not in the army. You don't have to 'yes sir' me each time I tell you something."

"Yes–" He caught himself and stopped.

Ryan suppressed a chuckle. "Do follow me to my study." He looked over the men. "I won't forget about you, either."

Ryan led the lieutenant down the hall. When they walked into the study, Meghan had already placed the coffee on the table and was on her way out the door.

"Meghan, make sure the men outside have some refreshments also."

"Yes, Papa."

As she walked out, Ryan noticed the young lieutenant sneaking a glance at her. As a father, he didn't know whether to be upset or pleased about that.

"So," Ryan asked, "have you men found quarters to stay until the shipment comes to Fall River?"

"If it's all right with you, sir, we were thinking of camping down where the railroad men used to be."

"I'm sure that can be arranged. You can use the main cabin. It has a telegraph to keep in touch with the train, to find out when it should arrive in Fall River."

"My thoughts exactly, si—Mr. Lochlan."

Ryan smiled at him. "You're learning, son."

The two sat in the study for some time as Meghan stood by the kitchen door, waiting to hear signs of when they would be leaving. She smoothed out her hair and her dress, hoping she looked okay.

Abby watched her while making apple pies. Her daughter seemed to have taken a fancy to the young man. Well, it was about time. After all, Meghan was going to be sixteen next year. Though Abby had never really worried, Meghan just seemed to have always marched to a different drummer.

Suddenly, the door opened, and Ryan and the lieutenant came out. Abby left the kitchen to talk to them.

"Lieutenant, I have made far too many pies for us here. Would you please take some of them for yourself and your men?"

The lieutenant was about to decline, but after one look at Abby's kind smile, he couldn't.

There was something about Abby—she had her late mother's trait of putting everyone at ease. He found it hard to say no to someone like that.

"It will be a pleasure, ma'am. It's been a long time since we've had any home cooking. I'll have one of the men come to the back and fetch them."

He nodded to Meghan as he followed Ryan to the front of the house, meeting her gaze just a second longer than was needed. "A lovely home you have here, Mr. Lochlan."

"Thank you. It was my wife's family home. Abby loves it here."

They walked out to the porch. The lieutenant noticed the roses, and a smile came to his face. "My mother had a rose garden in front of our home."

"Yes, my mother-in-law loved yellow roses, and Abby decided to keep the tradition. Where's your home, Lieutenant?"

"Oh, it's in a little place in Maine. Haven't seen it in over three years now."

"You should get back there one day. I myself miss my home, too."

"You are not from here, sir?"

Ryan smiled and shook his head. "You tell me you don't hear the accent, son? I was born and raised in Ireland."

"Forgive me, sir. It's just that, in Boston, everyone sounds like you, even the children."

Ryan thought about it and had to admit he was right.

"That's true, son. Forgive me. I forgot that."

The lieutenant turned to the sergeant. "Have one of the men go to the back of the house and take a basket from Mrs. Lochlan."

"Yes, sir. Corporal Todd, go fetch the basket from the missus, and be quick about it."

The young corporal ran to the back of the house.

"Sergeant, have the men mount."

"Yes, sir."

The young lieutenant mounted his horse as well, and they waited for the corporal to join them. The young man came running from the house with the basket. He passed it to one of the soldiers.

"Corporal Todd," the sergeant said. "Let's see you get your butt in the saddle. We haven't got all day."

The young man got on his horse, and the regiment started to move. Lieutenant Tucker smiled at Ryan and tipped his hat to Abby and Meghan.

Meghan watched them as they rode down the trail and turned onto the main road.

Abby wondered if maybe that was the young man who would catch her Meghan's eye and inspire her to be more of a lady.

A week later, Ryan invited the lieutenant for Sunday dinner. After church, Meghan was trying to decide which dress she was going to wear.

Her sister Molly came downstairs to the kitchen to complain to her mother. "Mama, you have to do something with Meghan. She's tried on five dresses so far and won't let me near the closet to get even one dress on."

"This is ridiculous," Abby mused. "It's not high tea with the Queen of England."

Abby left the kitchen, climbed the stairs to the girls' room, and knocked on the door. "Meghan, open this door."

She received no response.

"Meghan Catherine Lochlan, open this door now!"

Slowly, the door finally opened, and Meghan's innocent face appeared.

"Open it completely," Abby said.

Meghan obeyed, and Abby walked in. She looked around and saw dresses all over the beds and even the floor.

Abby looked back at her daughter. "I want this all cleaned up, and what you have on, you are wearing. The subject is closed."

"But Mama..."

"The subject is closed and not up for discussion."

Abby had set the dining room table elegantly. One would think the queen was really attending, but Abby thought since the young lieutenant hadn't been home in three years, giving him a bit of culture would give him something of what he remembered of his home.

She had Molly place a vase of roses on each end of the table, along with a centerpiece that had always been a favorite of her mother's: a silver candelabra. The young man came to the door not empty-handed.

Ryan answered the door. "Welcome, Lieutenant."

He walked into the house and was greeted by Abby in the foyer.

"Lieutenant Tucker," she said, "I'm so glad you agreed to have dinner with us."

"Ma'am, it was a pleasure to accept your invitation. Oh, I have gotten these for you—a small thank you for the pies and this lunch."

From under his arm, he handed Abby a beautifully wrapped box. Abby smiled and unwrapped the box to reveal a lovely lace shawl.

She placed the box on the hall table, took the shawl out, and wrapped it around her shoulders. "This is lovely. Thank you so much, but it wasn't necessary."

"I thought it was you when I saw it in the shop in town, ma'am."

"Well, I think it was sweet of you, and I may never take it off for the rest of the day."

She put her arm through the lieutenant's and escorted him to the dining room.

The first person he saw when he went in was Meghan. She looked beautiful in a hunter-green dress. It brought out the green in her eyes, although he could never place what color they were. He always thought they were a peculiar shade of gray.

All of Abby's daughters were beautiful in their own way, but he couldn't help but focus on Meghan.

"Hi," he said to the girls then met Meghan's eyes last, holding eye contact until she shyly looked away.

Michael smiled, knowing he had an effect on her.

They had a nice dinner, with Abby and Ryan leading the conversation. They asked him a dozen questions a minute, and Michael answered them enthusiastically, glad to boast of his achievements in front of such pretty ladies. Meghan hardly said two words, but he liked knowing that she was listening and that she was looking at him whenever he spoke.

When it came time for dessert, fresh apple pie, Abby turned to Ryan.

"Dear, I think maybe you and Lieutenant Tucker would like to retire to the study, and we girls can get this cleared up. If you like, I can have your coffee served on the porch."

"Yes, that would fine. Lieutenant, would you care to join me in the study?"

"Yes." He grinned.

The porch was set up for coffee and dessert. For the first time in a long time, the young lieutenant had been able to relax and enjoy a family meal and just to sit and smell the roses.

"I can't tell you how wonderful it was to have you here today," Abby said. "I do hope you will come again. We'd love to have you."

"That's very kind of you to say, Mrs. Lochlan. I had a wonderful time. And now, if you'll excuse me, I think it's time I start back for town."

He got up, and Ryan followed him to the end of the porch. Lieutenant Tucker mounted his horse and offered Ryan his hand.

"Mr. Lochlan, thank you for the invitation."

Abby came and stood by her husband. "Thank you for the lovely gift, Michael."

He smiled at them and tipped his hat as he slowly rode off. But at an inner urge, he stopped and turned, smiling at Meghan and the other girls. Then he continued down the road.

Abby wondered if he would be the first gentleman to catch her daughter's eye–and the last. After all, he was handsome and an officer. But it was still too soon to tell.

After he left the Lochlan farm, Lieutenant Tucker smiled as he remembered his evening with Meghan. She certainly had something that set her apart from her sisters, but he couldn't put his finger on it. Maybe it was those magnificent eyes of hers. He had never seen eyes that color.

Whatever color they were, they had a way of holding on to a man's mind and maybe even his heart.

CHAPTER TWO

Another week passed. A wire said the gold shipment was on its way down from Boston. Lieutenant Tucker rode out to the Lochlan farm to get Ryan.

Lieutenant Tucker and Ryan took no time in getting back in town. The train was sure to arrive at 3:15 p.m.

As the lieutenant and Ryan waited on the platform, a wire came for Ryan. It was from his friend Mick, who was also on the train.

"Where are your men stationed?" Ryan asked the lieutenant.

"Up and down the track. Is something wrong, Mr. Lochlan?"

He looked at the young man. "A friend of mine is also on the train. That means they're expecting trouble."

The lieutenant turned toward his men.

"Don't make them move. Leave them where there are for now. They are better off along the track right now. There will be people getting off the train. I don't want them in the line of fire."

As if on cue, the whistle sounded in the distance. Ryan turned and looked at the ship at the dock, which was waiting to be loaded. His orders were to make sure the gold was transported safely to the ship from the train for its trip to New York.

"You have that look in your eyes, Mr. Lochlan. Is something wrong?"

"Just a feeling, Lieutenant—just a feeling. Have some of your men move in."

The train pulled in slowly as they waited on the platform. It came to a stop, and a few passengers got off. Ryan walked down to the last car as it opened, and Mick stuck his head out the door.

"Hey Ryan!" he said.

"Mick, it's good to see you. Come on down. I want you to meet someone."

Mick jumped down off the car and gave Ryan a hug. "It's been a while. How's Abby and the kids?"

"They're great. This is Lieutenant Tucker. He's in charge of this whole shebang."

The lieutenant extended his hand to Mick. "Pleasure, *sir*."

Ryan smiled. "I forgot to tell you he has this thing about calling people sir."

"It's all right," Mick said. "I'm kinda used to hearing it back in DC."

"Mick, they call you sir?" Ryan asked.

"Yep. At first, I found it a bit strange, but now I'm used to it."

They went down to the dock and watched the gold being loaded onto the ship.

"So tell me, Mick," Ryan asked, "why all this for a gold shipment?"

Mick leaned in to the two men and said in a low voice, "It's all for show. The real gold is still on the train. What you see being loaded is a decoy."

"Expecting that much trouble?" Ryan asked.

"You never know with these stragglers and thieves. Better to be safe than sorry."

At the house, Abby was thrilled to see Mick. As he got off his horse, she jumped into his arms.

"Oh, Mick, it's so good to see you."

Mick beamed at her. "Well, if I knew I was going to get this reception, I would have come here sooner. How are you, beautiful? You're beautiful as ever."

"Fine. Wait till Holly hears you're here. She's with Mary, visiting old Mrs. Clark. Oh, both of them are going to be so glad to see you."

The lieutenant and Ryan were standing there watching the whole scene. Ryan cleared his throat, and Abby turned to him as if seeing her husband for the first time.

"Was there something you wanted, Ryan? Lieutenant Tucker, you are staying for supper. I will not hear any different."

"Yes, ma'am."

Abby truly did like the young man and hoped that Meghan felt the same way.

After dinner, Ryan and Mick retired to the study, and to his pleasure, the lieutenant found himself on the porch with Meghan.

Sitting on the porch swing was relaxing, especially since the young man wanted to ask Meghan something.

Before he could, Meghan noticed something in the sky. "There's a shooting star. Make a wish quick!"

"Make a wish?"

She looked at him. "Yes, it's what you do when you see a shooting star. Have you never heard of that?"

"Not really."

"Well, Lieutenant Tucker, let me tell you that when one sees a shooting star, they are to make a wish on it, and the wish will come true."

"Does it always work? I mean, does the wish always come true?"

She thought about that for a moment and then looked back at him. When she did, he was closer to her, so close she could feel him breathing. She felt excited–and lightheaded and intoxicated.

"Well, why you don't make a wish and wait and see," Meghan suggested, sounding a little shier.

"Maybe I should ask you a question first."

She turned to him, wondering what he could possibly ask.

"Miss Lochlan, would you do me the honor of accompanying me to the officer's ball in Somerset next week?"

Meghan sighed in relief. At first, she'd thought he was going to ask her something else. She smiled. "I would love to, Lieutenant."

The young man grinned from ear to ear as he stood up.

"You've made me so happy, Miss Lochlan."

"Lieutenant, don't you think we could call each other by our first names? I mean, after all, we are going to a ball together."

"Yes, yes you're right. Meghan, you have made me very happy."

"I'm glad, Michael. Now, see how easy that was?"

Still smiling, he sat back down again.

Not long thereafter, Ryan and Mick came out to the porch, and Meghan told her father of the ball that Michael asked her to.

Ryan turned to the boy. "Well, I think that is fine, Michael. May I call you Michael?"

"Yes, yes, sir... I mean, Mr. Lochlan."

"We'll work on that, but when you're ready, you can call me Ryan."

Michael stood up and headed for the front of the porch, holding Meghan's hand.

"Mr. Lochlan, Mr. Dawson, if you'll excuse me, I feel it's time I get back to town. I'll say good night to you now, and I'd like to say good night to Meghan privately, if you don't mind."

Both men nodded and watched as the new couple walked to the front of the house. Mick was the first to say something.

"Seems like our little girls are growing up."

"Seems that way, doesn't it?" Ryan didn't know whether he was sad or proud.

In the front yard, the lieutenant mounted his horse and smiled down at Meghan. "I had a wonderful time."

"So did I, Michael. Will I see you tomorrow?"

"I hope so. I'll let you know."

He gave her one last smile and rode down toward the main road.

She skipped back into the house and found her mother. "It's so wonderful! He asked me to the officer's ball. The officer's ball! Oh, that has to be like Cinderella going to the ball."

"What you are going to wear to the ball?" Abby teased. "Do we need to get glass slippers?"

"Well, if I can find them, I'll wear them." Meghan sighed again. "Isn't life just wonderful?"

"Yes, it is. To think, you are going to your first ball. How exciting!"

"Oh, it is, isn't it?"

Meghan floated up the stairs as if she had wings. Abby turned to Ryan as he walked back into the house.

"It seems the first of our little girls is growing up. Lieutenant Tucker has asked Meghan to her first officer's ball."

"So I've heard."

Abby put her arms around Ryan and squeezed him tightly.

"That explains the private goodbyes, holding hands."

"There's nothing to turn back time, is there?" Ryan asked.

"I'm afraid not." Abby smiled. "I'm happy for her, but I'm afraid she's growing into a young woman."

Ryan sighed. He turned back to Mick. "If you will excuse us, we old married folk will let you get some rest. Good night."

"Good night, Ryan," Mick said. "And you too, Abby."

Abby walked to their room with Ryan's arm around her waist.

At times, Mick envied Ryan. Even though he loved his wife Mary, Abby and Ryan's closeness was like nothing he had ever seen. He hoped he would have that love with Mary as they grew old together.

In their room, Ryan looked out at the clouds racing across the moon.

Abby walked up behind him and whispered in his ear, "It's the gypsy dancing in the twilight."

He turned, kissed her forehead, and said, "You know, you are the one dancing in the twilight. You are the gypsy that dances in my soul."

CHAPTER THREE

Meghan Lochlan was one of the prettiest girls at the ball. Well, in Michael's eyes she was, and from the looks she was getting, other officers seemed to feel the same way.

Dressed in a silver satin gown with chiffon wrist-length sleeves trimmed in rhinestones and a fitted bodice with rhinestones around the neckline, the color brought out the gray of her eyes. With the opera-length silver gloves, she actually felt like the belle of the ball.

Even thought it was her first ball, Meghan acted as though it was one of many she had attended. As she danced with many of the officers during the night, she had to sit a few out to breathe. Michael took her out the side doors on to the patio, where she was able to sit and catch her strength.

"I think we're causing a stir here on the dance floor," she remarked to Michael.

He leaned toward her and whispered into her ear, "The one they are looking at is you. You're the prettiest girl at this ball. All the other officers wish you were their dates."

He took her hand and led her back onto the dance floor. He twirled her, and she felt as if she was floating on the clouds.

"I'm having such a wonderful time," she said. "I don't want it to end."

He looked at her with a faint smile that Meghan found strange.

"Is there something wrong?"

"Well, I got my orders today. Seems they are transferring me out west to Fort Laramie. It's in Wyoming."

The music stopped—at least in Meghan's head. The lieutenant escorted her to the outside patio.

Once they were alone, she shot him a look. "Fort Laramie! Did you just find out?"

"Well, not really. I had asked for an assignment out west. The west is changing each day, and I really feel that if I want to become more than a lieutenant. I need to get more experience than guarding a gold shipment here in the east."

"Wyoming!" Meghan still couldn't believe it. "How can they do this?"

"Meghan, I'm sorry, but the army can do anything they want to. I belong to the army. Until my time with them is up, my time is with them."

She turned away, trying to hide her tears. When she reclaimed some strength, she faced him again. "What about us?"

He didn't respond right away, so she looked into his eyes for his answer.

"Michael, what about us?" she repeated.

He moved closer and looked into her eyes—eyes that were the true smoky gray of a storm cloud rushing across the sky before the rain comes.

"I'm very fond of you, Meghan," he said slowly and carefully, "and I think you're a beautiful girl. But I have to leave when I'm told to go. You can understand that, can't you? It's the life I chose, and a woman who cares for me will have to understand that."

She looked at him. The only thing she understood was that he was leaving her. And he would probably never see her again.

She gathered her courage and held her head high.

"Oh, I do understand, Lieutenant Tucker. I understand how you and others like you come to a town and lead young ladies on with false promises and leave them with broken dreams. Well, I assure you, Lieutenant Tucker, you will leave no broken dreams or heart here. And if you'd don't mind, I would like to be taken home now."

They spent the trip home in silence. When they reached the house, she was in such a rush to go home that she got out of the carriage unaided.

"I will say good night to you here. There is no need to take me to the door."

With that, she opened the door of the house and stormed in, refusing to look back at the young man, who was sitting in the carriage with his mouth hanging open in shock.

Days passed into weeks, and weeks turned into months after the day Lieutenant Tucker had left.

Meghan spent more time with her books. Her sisters began to get worried.

Brian and Nora Kelly, friends of the family, had been asking for the girls to come up and visit. Molly suggested taking Meghan, but their mother shot down the idea.

"But Mama, Meghan and I will be all right," Molly said. "We'll look after each other. We're so close."

"I know you and Meghan would love to be in Boston without a chaperone, but that, my dear girl, is not going to happen, no matter how close you say you are."

Since Lieutenant Tucker had left, Meghan and Molly had grown closer, attending dances together. Annie preferred to skip the dances and spend time with the animals. She had a gift with them, and they seemed to love and trust her.

Meghan did warm up to the idea of going to Boston and getting her mind off her heartbreak once and for all. Even though she didn't admit it to anyone, Lieutenant Tucker had hurt her.

Lucky for her, another opportunity to travel came. Their Aunt Mary invited both her and Molly to visit her in Washington with Mick and Holly. Aunt Mary's letter stated that she and Mick would meet them at the train station in

New York, and from there, they would head off to Washington.

Of course the girls were excited and counted the days until the excursion.

CHAPTER FOUR

The trip to Washington had its moments, good and bad. Seeing their cousin Holly again was one of the highlights of the trip, but being in the city of New York was an experience the girls really were not prepared for. The hustle and bustle of such a big city and its many people was simply too overwhelming for the village girls.

At least Meghan and Molly were able to enjoy the clothes shopping that Aunt Mary insisted on. Meghan thought it felt like Christmas Day with Aunt Mary just nodding for anything and everything the girls picked out. They would surely have to have most of the items shipped home or would need a car all to themselves, filled with packages. They even got a few things for Annie so she wouldn't feel left out.

Mary and Mick decided to treat their nieces to a dinner at the fanciest restaurant in New York. It was called Delmonico's.

"I feel like a princess here," Molly exclaimed after a handsome waiter had left her side.

Mary didn't want to spoil it by telling them everyone was treated that way at Delmonico's.

Meghan and Molly were both wearing lovely new dresses. Meghan's red dress compliment-ed her black hair, and she felt glamorous, like a true city girl.

The girls didn't lack attention. All the men had turned their heads when they walked in. Young, old, middle-aged—nearly every man noticed them. Holly was used to the attention, but her beautiful cousins found it flattering.

The girls wondered what it would be like in Washington. With all that they'd experienced in New York, they couldn't anticipate what awaited them in the nation's capital.

The train arrived at Union Station. After they stopped in Washington, Uncle Mick had them board a carriage. After a brief ride, they arrived at the front of the Dawson home.

When the carriage stopped, Meghan and Molly were able to look at the house. Large lion sculptures guarded the front doors. The entire house was made of stone, and the windows were diamond shaped. The house was one of the most beautiful, if not the most beautiful house, that the girls had ever seen. They were met by a maid and a butler as they all got out of the wagon.

Meghan couldn't believe Holly lived there. And Mary too. They both used to live with them at the farm. Mary was Abby's sister, Meghan's aunt. Now Mary was also Holly's stepmother since she married Mick after his divorce.

"Lilian, George, these are my nieces, Meghan and Molly," Mick said. "They will be with us for a few days, and I think the bedroom next to Miss Holly's would be suitable for them."

Lillian smiled. "Yes, Mr. Mick." She opened the door for Mary, and the girls followed her indoors.

"Lillian, I think the girls would like to freshen up before dinner, and they have a few dresses that will need to be pressed before they are hung in the closet, please."

"Yes, ma'am."

Lillian started up the stairs, and the girls followed. Holly was ahead of Meghan and Molly, to show them where their room was. She walked past her own room and opened the next door, to a larger bedroom containing two cozy beds and two chairs near a table.

"This is the guest room. It's bigger than most of the bedrooms except for Papa and Mary's. I'll let you get situated. When you're ready, just come over to my room."

With that, she was gone, and she closed the door behind her.

With wide eyes, Meghan looked at Molly and then at the room. "Can you believe this? Aunt Mary has a maid and a butler. Mama would never believe this if we tell her."

A knock on the door made the girls turn their heads. Lillian's voice called out, "I have some lemonade for you if you are thirsty."

Meghan answered the door. "Thank you, Lillian. This is very nice."

"If you need anything else, just call for me."

"Call for you?"

Lillian pointed to a tassel hanging down from the ceiling. "Just give one or two tugs on that, and I'll know you need me." She gave them a smile and headed back down the hall. Meghan looked at Molly again, incredulous, then took a sip of her lemonade.

"Well, shall we go and see Holly's room?"

They went out just in time to catch Aunt Mary coming up the stairs.

"Girls, is everything all right?" she asked.

Molly answered first. "Oh, everything is fine, Aunt Mary. We were just going over to see Holly's room. She told us to meet with her after we got settled in."

"I see. Well, I'll see you both at dinner, then."

Mary continued to her room, and the girls arrived at Holly's room door and lightly tapped on it.

Holly called from the inside, "Come on in."

Molly opened the door and couldn't believe her eyes. Holly's room was large, larger than the room they'd all shared back at home during their childhood years in Fall River. With pink flowered wallpaper and a bed cover and curtains to match, Meghan thought it was the girliest looking room she'd ever seen.

"Molly, come on in. I'll be right with you. Just fixing my hair."

Holly appeared from a door that led to a private sitting room, which Molly had thought was a closet. Holly had changed into a beautiful pink dress, and her hair hung down around her shoulders.

"So do you two like your room? If not, we have two others."

Meghan was still in awe of Holly's room as she looked around. "No, it's fine, Holly... just fine."

"Good, because I want you both to have a great time while you're here. I even plan on having Mary work on Aunt Abby, to have you girls come back and go to school here in Washington. Think of how much fun we will have being together again."

She gave them a hug. Going to school there in Washington was not something the girls had been planning or even thinking of. Meghan doubted her mother would consider sending them away to Washington for their schooling. A *visit was different, but to live away from home?* Anyway, she would worry about that another time. They were there to enjoy the week with their cousin.

Dinner was served at six, and the girls were instructed that they had no excuse for tardiness. Another must was that everyone had to be dressed for dinner. The reason was one never knew who would show up at the door, and one should always look one's best under any circumstances.

The main dining room was massive, and it made the Lochlan sisters' dining room back in Fall River look more like a closet in comparison.

Mary greeted them.

"Is your room all right, girls? I can always have you moved to another."

"No, it's beautiful," Meghan said. "This house is so huge."

"Yes, it is a bit large, but Mick got it at a good price, and we love the neighborhood. I'll introduce you to the neighbors tomorrow morning at church."

Mick smiled at the girls. "I can't tell you how glad I am that your folks allowed you to come for a visit. I've been trying to get your folks to come here for over a year now. They always seem to have something else that needs them back at home. I'm hoping that you will tell them how they can surely take a few days off and come here and relax a bit."

"Well, I know we can tell them, Uncle Mick, but I can't promise they will come," Meghan said.

They all laughed at that, knowing she was right. Both parents were hard to convince that the farm could run without them for a few days.

The rest of dinner went on with the usual conversation, talk about current events and Aunt Mary telling Holly she would be expected to introduce the girls to some of the girls at the various dances.

"You girls do like dances, don't you?"

"Of course we do, Aunt Mary."

"Good." She smiled.

Lillian came into the dining room and announced to Uncle Mick that someone was here to see him.

"Sir, a Mr. Feeny would like to speak to you. I arranged for him to see you in your library."

"Thank you, Lillian." He turned back to his wife and the girls. "If you'll excuse me, I have to speak with this man." He got up and left the dining room.

Mary explained, "This happens at least twice a week, that we at times have only two at this dinner table."

"There are times we don't see Father until the next day," Holly added.

"Well, Uncle Mick does have an important job," Molly said.

Holly began to nod but then turned to Mary to say, "You know, sometimes I wish we were still living at Fall River. At least we were all together."

Aunt Mary sighed in longing.

CHAPTER FIVE

Aunt Mary and Holly introduced Meghan and Molly to some of the most notable families in Washington, and there wasn't a social event that they were not invited to.

Aunt Mary took the girls to some of the historical places in Washington. They even had a tour of the Senate and the Hall of Congress. Mary wanted the girls to be exposed to the importance of these sights. She took them to Arlington, where they paused to honor the brave men who'd fought to keep the country free.

Mick also got involved in taking the girls around. He took them to the White House, although only the outside. Nonetheless, they got to see where their president lived.

Everyone Holly knew wanted to meet her cousins. Holly hadn't planned on that, and she wasn't sure how she felt about it. She was used to being the center of attention, but her two cousins became the talk of Washington.

Meghan caught the eye of many of the young men, and her dance card was often filled, most of the time before the second dance.

During one gala, Meghan caught the eye of a handsome young man named Adam Bradford. He was an aide to a congressman from Pennsylvania.

He was captivated by Meghan, who was smiling and immediately capturing the heart of every young man there.

As she danced in the arms of another aide, Adam slowly found his way to the outside patio. He felt he would not have a chance to dance with her at all, and the hall was getting stuffy.

The evening air was warm, and the smell of roses filled the air on the patio. The young aide looked out over the patio and watched the moon as clouds floated by it. Suddenly, he heard a voice behind him.

"You know, when the clouds race across the moon like that, it's known as the gypsy dancing in the moonlight."

He turned at the sound of a sweet young woman's voice. "Pardon?"

"It's true. It's called a gypsy dancing in the moonlight. I suppose you never heard it, have you?"

He could only smile at her. He found it hard to believe that the most beautiful woman, whom he'd been admiring all evening, was less than ten feet away from him. "No, I have never heard that."

"My mama's mama told her that when she was a young girl."

"I see... and your mother's mother had this on good authority?"

"Well, of course."

She moved closer toward a large stone and sat up on it. She took her shoes off and put them on top of the ledge.

"I'm sorry, but I've been dancing for so long I just had to take some time off my feet. You don't mind if I sit here for a bit, do you? I don't like wearing these shoes. I don't like wearing any kind of shoes. I prefer wearing boots."

He had to smile again as he watched her dangling her feet in the air.

"Who are you here with?" he asked her.

"Well, my sister and cousin are in there, and I expect they can handle the rest of the dancing for the time being."

"Your sister and cousin?"

"Yes, my cousin Holly Dawson. Maybe you know my Uncle Mick? Mick Dawson."

Just then, Holly and Molly came outside looking for Meghan. They found her talking to the handsome young man.

"Meghan, we were wondering what happened to you," Holly scolded.

"Well my feet were hurting, so I came out here and found this gentleman." She turned back to him. "You know, I never got your name."

He smiled and bowed gracefully. "Bradford, Adam Bradford at your service, Miss..."

"Meghan Lochlan. It is a pleasure to meet you, Mr. Bradford."

"Believe me, the pleasure was mine, Miss Lochlan."

"Meghan it's time to go," Holly said. "And for goodness sake, put your shoes on."

"I will, Holly. Just give me a minute."

Holly looked at Adam and smiled. She had to admit he was rather handsome—sandy blond hair and blue eyes, a smile that seemed to feel he was laughing with you, not at you. She wondered why she hadn't seen him before.

As the girls made their way back into the hall and toward the foyer, to get their shawls and leave, Holly took another look back at Mr. Bradford. She would not forget that face the next time.

For the next few days, the talk of the Dawson home was Meghan sitting outside the hall with no shoes on, talking to some congressman's aide. Holly found it an unsuitable thing for a young lady to do.

"Mary, tell her how wrong it was to be sitting on the ledge, dangling her feet in the air. Why, it was like some common washwoman."

Mary gave Holly a sharp look after that remark. "And tell me what was so wrong, Holly? Meghan was not inside the hall, and who saw it was—if I can recall—you, Molly, and that Mr. Bradford."

"But Mary, if any of my friends—"

"Holly, if any of your friends have anything to say, I hope you have the good sense to tell them that she is your cousin and to defend her actions. Let's not forget that her parents took you in when you had nowhere to go. Do I make myself clear, Holly?"

"Yes, ma'am."

The rest of their stay at their aunt's was confined to socials and teas with their aunt. Holly spent less and less time with the girls. She was often out with friends or entertaining a certain gentleman. Meghan and Molly were never invited.

So came the end of their visit. Uncle Mick planned to accompany them back to Fall River. He had to go on a business trip anyway. The girls said their goodbyes to their aunt and Holly at the station.

"Girls, tell your mother that we'll be there for your eighteenth birthday party," said Mary. "Give your folks a hug for me, and I want Annie to come with you next time."

The girls took their turns hugging their aunt.

"Aunt Mary, thank you so much for a wonderful time," Meghan said. "We'll miss you."

"Meghan, you take your shoes off anytime you want. Don't let anyone tell you different."

"Thanks for letting us stay," Molly said as she embraced her aunt.

Holly hugged them next. "Come back soon!"

Meghan wondered if she meant it.

Mick helped his nieces board the train. They made their way to their car and waved out the window as the train left the station. Mick took a seat across from them.

Molly turned to her sister. "Do you think you'll ever see that Bradford gentleman again?"

"Oh, I don't think so, Molly. After all, I was only talking to him for that short time. I'm sure he has other things on his mind than a girl who takes her shoes off. Besides—" Meghan stopped and shook her head, thinking better of discussing something that involved Mick's daughter.

Mick looked at his two grown-up nieces and shook his head. He felt as if it was only yesterday that they'd been born, and in only a few months, they would be eighteen years old.

"If you like, Meghan, I can find out a bit about him," he offered.

"Thanks, but I really feel I'd like to remember it as a chance meeting."

Meghan didn't want to tell him that Holly had already found out about him and was planning to ask him to the July Fourth dance at the capitol in two weeks.

CHAPTER SIX

Meghan and Molly were happy and relieved to be back home in Fall River. Mary had sent with the girls a note asking Abby to consider sending all three of her daughters to Washington to enroll in Miss Cartwright's Finishing School. As the note stated, the school was one of the most prestigious in Washington for girls of fine families, and Mary said it would be wonderful for the girls to have a real education.

Abby reread that line again. The girls had gone to school until they were ten and then were homeschooled as Abby and her sisters had been. After all, in those days, it was normal for girls to learn the basics.

Their mother had done a fine job with her girls. Abby looked around the study, remembering how her mother had spent hours with the girls, teaching them in there. She could still see Mary and Little Annie sitting on the floor as her mother would read to all four of them. Whenever Abby thought of those memories, tears rolled down her face.

A moment later, Ryan came into the room and saw his wife crying.

"What's wrong?"

"It's Mary. She wants us to send the girls to Washington to some finishing school for young girls of fine families."

He walked over and sat down beside her. "Well, do you want to send the girls?"

"I really don't want to, but Mary says it will be the best for them if they want to become part of society."

"Abby, there is nothing wrong with our girls' education. They were taught by one of the best teachers I know."

He gently kissed her cheek.

"Thank you."

Abby looked across the room at the painting above the mantel, which depicted Abby and the children sitting on the porch in front of the house. She had given it to Ryan for his birthday.

As she looked at the painting of her smiling children, tears filled her eyes again. Ryan had never seen his Abby like that. She had always been the strong one. Sometimes he had to be reminded that she needed to have someone to lean on during tough times.

"Abby, you're just like every other mother who doesn't want to see her children grow up. But don't worry, they are not leaving yet. You'll still have the girls here for a bit longer, and let's not forget we still have the boys. Come on, let's go get you some rest, and all this will look better in the morning."

Slowly, she got up, and he took her to their room. As she lay beside him, his arm draped over her, she fell into a peaceful sleep, free of worry about the girls.

Ryan was right. Everything did look better in the morning.

Two months passed after that night, and nothing more was said.

In the early summer, the Churchill family moved to Fall River. They opened a hotel and restaurant in town.

On the parcel of land they purchased from the railroad, they erected a lovely two-story building, a restaurant and hotel that served not only those passengers from the train but also those coming in from the ships that docked down by the river.

The Churchill House had all the charm and beauty of many of the hotels one would find in the big cities such as New York or Boston. For this reason, Abby considered having the girls' eighteenth birthday party there. Although her home was adequate, their birthday was an important milestone for the girls, and she knew a lot of guests would be attending.

On a warm summer morning, Abby arrived at the front of the Churchill House and met a friendly woman with silver-blond hair and rosy cheeks.

"Welcome to the Churchill house," Alice Churchill said.

Samuel helped Abby off her carriage and then tended to the horse.

"Thank you," she replied. "I'm Abby Lochlan. I spoke to your husband about holding a birthday party here."

"Yes. Please, do come in."

Alice showed her in the front door. As soon as she entered, Abby gasped at the ambience of the interior. The front hall was massive and elegantly decorated, with rich upholstered furniture and crystal chandeliers over the front desk. A thick navy carpet covered the floor, and grand stairs led to the rooms on the second floor. The colors of the front room included a rich, deep blue that carried to the curtains, giving the entire room a regal look.

Alice smiled at Abby. "As you can see, this is the front hall. We made sure it would make a good impression. Those stairs lead you to the second floor, where we have eighteen rooms and two suites. There are three baths situated—two are upstairs, and one is down here for the clients who are using the dining room. If you follow me this way, I'll take you to the dining room."

She opened the massive French-type doors, revealing another huge room. She walked into the room that, like the front room, was also elegantly furnished. The tables were covered in white linen tablecloths and napkins. The centerpiece for each table was a single candle in a fluted glass holder, to add to the touch of intimate dining. The chairs were upholstered like the furniture outside, except the color scheme in this room was a deep emerald green.

"We also have a large patio past those doors on the far right if you care to use it for dancing," Alice added. "My husband mentioned you were planning a birthday party for an eighteen-year-old girl?"

"Yes, our girls are going to be eighteen next month, and we wanted to give them something special."

"Twins, how lovely."

Abby suppressed a chuckle. "No, triplets. We have three daughters."

"Three girls!" Alice exclaimed. "Oh, this is a cause for a special celebration. Don't worry. It will be perfect."

She pulled a chair out from a nearby table and asked Abby to sit. Alice took a pencil and a pad to jot down ideas for the celebration.

"Now, I'm thinking the theme will have to be in threes, and the girls will have the table in the center since they are the guests of honor. I think you and Mr. Lochlan may want to sit to their right with other members of the family. Do you have other children, Abby?"

"Yes, twin boys."

Alice looked up from her notes. "Triplets and twin boys. I must say, you had your hands full."

"Yes, I did." Abby laughed.

They continued to plan the event. After half the afternoon, Abby and Alice had decided on what they were going to do for the party. As Abby walked back to the carriage, Jake Rooney approached her.

"I'm glad I caught up with you, Mrs. Lochlan. Here's your mail. There's a letter for Mr. Lochlan from the railroad. I thought it may be important."

"Why, thank you, Jake. Alice, have you met our postal clerk? This is Jake Rooney, Jake, this is Alice Churchill. She and her husband Samuel own the new hotel in town."

"We've met," Jake said. "Mrs. Churchill, by the way, the seven fifteen train will be on time, ma'am."

"Our son Christian is coming for a visit," Alice explained. "He's at medical school in New York."

"At Bellevue? Oh, that's a wonderful college."

"Oh, yes, it is, but it's so far away. I wish he had chosen Harvard."

"We mothers are all alike. We want to keep our children close. Sometimes we have to let them go. Is he your only child?"

"We also have an older daughter who lives in New York. He and her husband own a bakery there. She's promised to supply us with the baked goods when we open up. Her husband is an artist. He's good at decorating cakes. I want him to do a special one for your girls."

As Abby rode back to the farm, she grew more excited about the girls' party. She was glad to have met Alice Churchill, and she couldn't wait to show her daughters the hotel.

When she arrived home, she found Ryan sitting on the porch steps.

He got up and helped her down from the carriage. "Where have you been all day, my love?"

"I went to meet the Churchills. I spoke to Alice, at least. We're having the girls' party there next month."

"Oh?"

"Yes, it's perfect, and they have plenty of room, and the best part is I don't have to clean up."

"I see, and who is going to pay for this gala event?"

"We are, of course, with the money we are saving by not sending the girls to that fancy school in Washington."

He leaned down and kissed her lightly on the forehead. "Did I ever tell you how much I love you?"

"Every day, but I never get tired of hearing it." She reached over and took some packages from the back of the carriage, as well as the mail. "Oh, I almost forgot, there's a letter here from the railroad for you."

"The railroad?"

She handed him the letter along with the other packages and went into the house. As she went through the mail, she saw one for Meghan. The return address was Fort Laramie.

"Meghan!" she called.

Rustling came from the second floor, and Meghan appeared at the top of the staircase. "Yes, Mama?"

"You have a letter here."

She wondered who could have written a letter to her. Maybe it was Holly, writing to apologize for being so catty the day they left. She came down the stairs and saw the letter on the table near the stairs. Slowly, she picked up the envelope and noticed the return address was from Fort Laramie. She sat on the stairs and opened the envelope.

Dear Meghan,

I hope this letter finds you and your family in good health. We arrived here at Fort Laramie a few months ago. It's very different from life back east. It seems our main duties are to protect the settlers from the Indians and to keep the telegraph wires up. Col. Benten seems to feel we will be protecting the Pony Express riders as they make their way from St. Jose to California. We're a long way from home, but we're doing what we wanted.

I wanted you to know that I got married out here, Meghan. Col. Benton's daughter, Kate. I guess it was more or less love at first sight, and well, I wanted to let you know and hoped you would be happy for me.

Well, I guess I should end this letter now and wish you and your family well.

Sincerely,

Captain Michael Tucker

Meghan looked at the letter, absolutely stunned.

"Married! He sends me a letter to tell me he's married. Did he think I would sit here and pine away for him? As if I would wait for him like he was some big hero!"

She left the letter on the stairs and headed out the back door, toward the stable. Abby walked into the hall and noticed the letter on the stairs. She picked it up, read it, and then folded it to put it back in the envelope.

She looked out the back door and noticed the stable door was open.

Inside the stable, Meghan was talking to Gypsy, her copper-colored palomino with a golden mane and tail. She'd had Gypsy since she was a filly and raised her to be a fine riding horse.

Meghan took a comb and began grooming and talking to her. "Ya know, Gypsy, I don't know why I'm even upset about this. After all, we never really were a couple. There was nothing definite there. He took me to a ball, but there was nothing else. You don't even know what I'm talking about, do you?"

From behind her, she heard, "No, but I do."

Meghan turned and saw her mother standing at the door. Abby walked over to her daughter.

"I'm sorry, Meghan. I know you're hurt by this letter."

"Mama, he never even asked me what I thought. He just said he got his orders and he was leaving. And sending me this letter... Did he think I was waiting here for him to come back?"

Abby could see the tears in her daughter's eyes and would have done anything to take them away, but heartbreak was part of growing up.

She did hope it would be the last hurt Meghan would have to go through, but the future was never certain. She put her arm around Meghan.

After Meghan placed the brush back in a bucket, she walked back to the house with Abby. As they got to the back door, they saw Ryan.

"I was wondering where you two headed off to."

"We just needed a little mother-daughter time," Abby said.

"Oh?"

"Yes, and that's all you need to know."

CHAPTER SEVEN

Early the following morning, Samuel Churchill came riding up the road in his wagon. On the top-floor porch, Meghan and Molly were cleaning the window. It was time for some spring cleaning, and the girls were in charge of the outside while Annie and Abby were in charge of the insides of the windows. Abby noticed Samuel first as he got down from his wagon and walked to the door.

Abby walked to the door and opened it to welcome him. "Good morning, Samuel. Do come in."

"My son Christian is in the wagon."

"Well, bring him in."

Sam motioned for Christian to come down, and the young man got off the wagon. Even Abby was taken by surprise at the sight of the young, handsome blond man.

Abby smiled at him. "Come on in, Christian. It's nice to have you here."

The young man's face lit up as he walked up the front steps. Meghan and Molly tried to get a better look at him from the upstairs porch.

"You look a lot like your mother," Abby remarked, "but I imagine you're told that all the time."

"Yes, ma'am."

Abby smiled at Samuel and then back at Christian. "Please come in."

She escorted them into the house and to the living room.

"Make yourself comfortable, and I'll get my husband."

Christian looked around the room. It had a nice warm touch to it. He noticed a number of photographs on the mantel, all wedding photographs. One older photograph was of Mrs. Lochlan and three other women with the same man.

Abby came back into the room. "Ryan will be with you in a few minutes. He's getting washed up."

She noticed Christian was still looking at the photographs.

"I see you're looking at the family photos. That's my ma and pa, my sister Jenny, and my baby sister Mary."

Christian kept looking at more of the photos, then he turned to Abby. "Did your sisters marry twin brothers?"

"No, it's the same man. My sister Jenny was killed in a train accident, and Mick then married my sister Mary after a while."

Samuel shook his head at his son. "Christian! I'm sorry, Abby. He knows better than to ask personal questions."

"Oh, don't scold the boy for asking a question, Samuel. Besides, I don't mind answering something as innocent as that. Christian, you can ask me anything you like. If I can answer, I'll let you know."

She smiled at the boy, and he smiled back as Ryan came in.

"Samuel, good to see you again," Ryan said.

"Ryan, this is my son, Christian."

"Christian."

"Sir."

Meghan and Molly were in the kitchen when Abby went in.

"Mama," Molly said, "who's that?"

"It's Mr. Churchill and his son, Christian."

"Oh."

She looked at both the girls, anticipating the next question, but none came.

"Did you girls finish the windows in the downstairs porch?"

"Not yet."

"Well, you might want to start them now before lunch."

"Yes, Mama," Meghan said.

She grabbed Molly, and they headed off to the front of the house. They started in the dining room, with Meghan outside, where she had the perfect spot to see the young man. He did look their way a few times, and Meghan acted as though she was busy cleaning the window.

After the men finished their conversation and were heading toward the front door, Abby walked over to them.

"Do tell Alice I will be in town tomorrow, and Christian, it was a pleasure to meet you."

"My pleasure, Mrs. Lochlan."

As they headed out the door, Christian smiled at Meghan and Molly. He got in the wagon, and his father drove down the road toward the main road and town. Abby turned to her husband.

"You and Samuel sure were busy discussing something."

"Well, Samuel was interested in having another road to get to the hotel. He wanted a back way so that people from the docks need not climb the road to get up to town. I can see his point but explained that he would need someone who had surveyed that land. I told him that the man he should see is Mick Dawson. Mick knows that area better than I do."

"Can Mick take the time off from his work?"

"I don't know, but I did tell Samuel I would send a wire off to Mick in the morning."

Meghan and Molly exchanged glances. They both knew that could mean Aunt Mary and Holly would be joining Uncle Mick.

Abby looked at her daughters and then waited for Ryan to leave before she went to talk to them. The girls were starting to clean the last window when Abby spoke.

"Girls, I noticed you were not too pleased when your father mentioned he was going to wire Uncle Mick. Is there some reason you weren't all over him, asking him to invite Holly to come with him?"

The girls looked at each other.

"I'm waiting."

Meghan wanted to tell her, but she couldn't bring herself to say a word. Molly spoke up instead.

"Well, Mama, Holly's changed. She's not like the Holly you knew."

"That's right, Mama. And please don't send us away to that school. The girls are rude and cruel to other girls. We don't want to be like them. Mama, please don't send us."

Their voices could be heard in the kitchen, where Annie was washing dishes, and she came out to ask what was wrong. She found both her sisters in tears. "What happened, Mama?"

"All I know is they don't want to go to the school in Washington that Holly goes to." Abby looked back at her girls. "Is this true?"

They both nodded. She gave them each a hug, including Annie.

"You two could have told me. I was worried you both wanted to go. Your Aunt Mary said you had a wonderful time, and I thought when she suggested you both should go there, I thought that you really wanted to leave home and go live there."

She stepped back and looked at her girls.

Meghan looked down. "I'm sorry, Mama. We didn't want to speak badly about Holly. She's our cousin, after all."

Later that evening when the children were in bed, Abby was sitting at her dressing table, brushing her hair sitting when Ryan came in.

"Did you check the back door?" she asked.

He walked over and kissed her on the forehead. "Checked the doors, the windows, the boys who fell asleep with their clothes on, so I just put a cover over them."

She looked up at him and smiled. "They are a handful."

"Well, the girls at their age weren't so innocent if you remember. Meghan had me go to every horse farm to find that perfect horse for her. She fell in love with a scrummy little filly, and she just had to have her."

"Yes, but look at her today. You have to admit Gypsy is a beautiful horse."

Ryan started taking off his boots.

"Ryan?" Abby said.

"Hum."

"The girls really didn't like being at Mary and Mick's."

"Oh?"

"They don't like Holly's friends or Holly."

"Well, that's not like our girls. Holly's their cousin. They grew up together. What happened?"

"I don't know, Ryan. They seemed very upset and begged me not to send them to that school."

He walked over to her and took the brush out of her hand.

"We'll talk about this tomorrow. It's time for bed now."

"But I think we should talk about this now."

"Abby, do you feel that strongly enough that I have to lose much-needed sleep?"

"I really feel we need to discuss this, Ryan."

Ryan turned back to her. "Okay."

CHAPTER EIGHT

A week had passed since Christian had been to the Lochlan farm with his father, but he still remembered the daughter with the dark hair and the light eyes. He had never seen eyes that color before. They were all he could speak of to his mother. Were they gray? A light blue? He couldn't figure it out.

He was helping her mother hang the grand-opening banner when Abby and her children drove into town.

As they passed by the hotel, Abby and at the girls smiled and waved at them.

Alice smiled. "Morning, Abby."

"Morning, Alice, Christian."

Alice turned to her son. "Yes, I can see all three girls are very pretty."

Christian just looked at his mother, hoping she wouldn't say anything more, then continued hanging the banner. The Lochlan boys jumped off the carriage before their mother could get them.

"Thomas, Daniel, you are to go straight to Mr. Loring's to get haircuts. No stopping for candy. And don't come back without a haircut."

"But, Mama..."

"No buts. I want you to get haircuts, and that's final."

The three girls slowly got out of the carriage and followed their mother down to the Churchill House. Abby gave a big hug to Alice and Christian.

"Alice, Christian, I'd like to you to meet my girls. This is Meghan, Molly, and Annie."

Alice smiled at them. "I'm happy to meet you girls, finally."

Alice examined Meghan. "My, you do have beautiful eyes." Then she stopped and turned to the other two. "I'm sorry, I mean you girls all have beautiful eyes."

Molly stopped her. "It's all right, Mrs. Churchill, we're used to it. Meghan does have these strange-colored eyes. Our pa says his mother had the same color eyes."

Alice relaxed and smiled again. "Well your ma has planned to have your party here. Would you like to go in and see what it looks like?"

"Oh, yes, please," Annie said.

"Christian, would you like to show the girls inside and around the place?"

"Sure, Mother."

He made his way down the ladder with ease and landed on the porch of the hotel.

"Ladies." He smiled, almost shyly, and graciously showed them inside. "This is the main lobby, and straight through those doors is the restaurant."

He led them through the doors. The girls were very impressed with the room's beautiful decor, and they pointed out furniture and art to each other.

"Just outside is the patio, which can be used for dancing."

"Do you dance, Christian?" Molly asked coyly.

"Yes, yes I do. Do you?"

Molly began to blush and looked down. In almost a whisper, she replied, "Yes, I do."

"Can we see the patio, Mr. Churchill?" Annie asked.

He obliged and opened another set of doors.

"Sure, but the name is Christian. Mr. Churchill is my father."

He gave her a softer smile. Annie was the most gentle of the girls, and she had an innocent sweetness to her.

He opened the doors, and Annie rushed out onto the patio. All around, flowers were starting to bloom. By the next month, the entire backyard would be filled with roses, daisies, and scrubs. It truly was a magical setting for the party. Why, all that was needed was a handsome prince—no, three handsome princes for the Lochlan triplets.

"Oh, Meg, isn't it just beautiful?" Annie said to Meghan. "I can see it now—almost like a fairy tale."

Christian walked over to Annie and bowed slightly.

"May I have the honor of this dance?"

Annie curtsied and placed her hand in his, and they gently waltzed around the patio. The look on Annie's face was priceless. She was practically glowing.

After a while, Molly walked up and tapped her on the shoulder. "May I cut in?"

Annie bowed and stepped back so her sister could dance with Christian.

"You dance very well," Annie told him.

"Thank you, and you're not bad yourself."

Christian and Molly swirled around the patio as Meghan and Annie watched. Alice and Abby came out to the patio as well.

"I told you it would be wonderful for dancing," Alice said to Abby.

Abby watched Annie smiling as she watched Molly dancing while Meghan only showed a halfhearted interest.

"Well, girls, how do you like it?" Alice asked them.

Molly answered first. "It's lovely, Mrs. Churchill."

Annie was still in awe of the magic and the waltz. "It's a fairy tale come to life."

All eyes then fell on Meghan as they waited for her comment, but she really had nothing more to add. She thought it was a lovely restaurant, and it made her mother happy, and therefore, it made her happy.

"It's great," she finally said.

"I think it will do nicely for the party," Alice said. "Have you gone over the details such as the guest list, the food, and the band?"

Abby had forgotten those details. She was too busy admiring the restaurant.

"Mrs. Churchill, if you give me a day, I will have your guest list for you. I'll leave the food and the band to you."

Alice smiled at the girls. "Why, I could use all three of you to work here. I would have three of the prettiest waitresses anywhere."

Meghan considered it but ultimately said, "I can't speak for my sisters, Mrs. Churchill, but I have to decline the offer. Thank you for considering me."

Her sisters told Alice that they would think about it.

They all started toward the main lobby in the front, and Ryan came in with the twin boys.

"Seems these two handsome young men claim to be our sons," he said. "I told them that our sons had hair down to their shoulders like girls."

Daniel groaned.

Ryan and Abby laughed.

"Alice, these are our sons Daniel and Thomas." Abby said.

Alice couldn't get over the boys' hair, which was the color of autumn wheat, their soft brown eyes, and the sprinkle of freckles across their noses. She had to admit they were handsome, as handsome as her own son.

"I'm happy to meet you," she said.

"Thank you, ma'am."

Meghan went up to them. "Come on, you two, let's see if Mrs. Dixon has any new candy in her store."

Alice watched as Meghan led the boys down the street.

Ryan turned to Alice. "Could you tell Samuel that I got a wire from Mr. Dawson? He'll be here by the end of the week to talk with him."

"Thank you, Mr. Lochlan."

"Mick will be coming alone," he told Abby. "Mary is expecting, and the doctors don't advise her to travel at this time."

"And Holly?"

"Mick says Holly's at school. We'll talk more at home."

"Alice, I hope you don't mind if we leave," Abby said.

"Don't be silly. I understand it's a family matter. If you need anything, just let us know."

"Thank you."

"Mr. Lochlan, I don't know how to thank you for your help."

"Well, you can call me Ryan, for a start."

Alice smiled. "And you can call me Alice."

Three days had passed when a train pulled into Fall River. Only one passenger got off: Mick Dawson. He hadn't told Ryan what train he was taking and when he was coming.

He made his way down the platform and then the sidewalk toward the hotel. When he walked into the main lobby, Alice greeted him.

"Good afternoon. May I help you?"

Mick looked down at the registry and took the pen to sign his name.

"Yes, I'm Mick Dawson. I'd like a room, and I would like to speak with Samuel Churchill."

Alice smiled as she looked at his signature. "Yes, we can arrange both of those for you, Mr. Dawson. If you'll just excuse me for a moment, I'll get my husband."

Alice slipped inside the door behind the desk and got Christian.

"I need you to go to the dock and get your father. Tell him Mr. Dawson is here. Then go to the Lochlan farm and tell Mr. Lochlan."

"Yes, Ma."

She appeared back at the front desk, where Mick was waiting.

"Mr. Dawson, my husband will be here in a few moments. In the meantime, would you like to go to your room? I'll have my husband call for you when he comes in."

"That would be fine."

"That will be room ten, third door on the right. It's at the top of the stairs."

Mick took the key and thanked her.

Christian got to the Lochlan farm and knocked just as the family was about to have lunch. Meghan answered the door to find Christian standing there.

"Yes?" she asked in surprise.

"Miss Lochlan, my mother told me to tell your father that Mr. Dawson is at our hotel."

Meghan smiled. "Won't you come in? You can tell my father yourself. We're all in the dining room. Follow me."

She led him through the hall and into the dining room. "Papa, Christian Churchill's here to see you."

Ryan stood up from his chair. "Come in. Have a seat. Would you like something to eat?"

"No, thank you," he answered. "Sir, my ma told me to tell you that Mr. Dawson is down at the hotel."

"I see."

Abby looked at Ryan. "Mick is at the hotel?"

"Yes ma'am, he's in room ten," Christian said.

"Tell your ma thank you and I'll see both of them soon."

"Yes sir, Mr. Lochlan."

"Why didn't he come here first?" Abby asked Ryan.

"You know Mick, he probably wants to get business out of the way first." He turned to his daughter. "Meghan, would you like to show Christian the way to the door?"

"Yes, Papa."

Christian followed her out of the dining room and toward the front hall. She opened the front door for him. "Thank you for coming to tell my father."

"Meghan?" he said gently.

"Yes?"

"We're having a grand opening on Saturday. Do you think you could be there?"

"That would depend if my parents are coming into town."

Mesmerized by her eyes, he was unable to look away. "I'd like to have a dance with you."

She looked at him as if she didn't understand. "Pardon?"

"Well, I've danced with your sisters, and I'd like to see if you dance as well as your sisters."

"Mr. Churchill, is this some sort of game to you?"

"No, I'm only asking for a dance."

"Like I said, I'd go to see if my parents are going."

He smiled. "I hope they are."

She smiled back at him. "Good day, Mr. Churchill."

"Good day, Miss Lochlan."

Meghan watched him as he mounted his horse and rode down the road. She could see he wasn't used to riding. He sat very rigid on the saddle, stiff and almost afraid to move.

She closed the door and walked back to the dining room. She sat back down at the table and ate the rest of her lunch in silence.

Abby looked over at Meghan, but she had her head down.

CHAPTER NINE

Back in town, Mick was in the dining area when Samuel came in.

"Mr. Dawson."

Mick stood up from the table and extended his hand.

"Yes, Mr. Churchill, am I correct? I was told by Mr. Lochlan about your idea. I must say I haven't been on that trail for a good many years, but I'd be happy to help you."

Mick sat back down as Samuel pulled out a chair.

"I'm so glad I can get you to help," Samuel said.

"Can I get you anything?" Mick chuckled. "Look at me, offering to get you something when this is your place!"

"Well, yes, I would like some coffee. Alice?"

Alice came by. "Did you want something, Samuel?"

"I'd like some coffee, please."

"Oh, Mr. Dawson, we're having our grand opening tomorrow," Alice said. "I do hope you will join the luncheon in the afternoon."

"Well, how can I refuse such a wonderful invitation?" Mick said.

"We'll look forward to seeing you at the luncheon."

She smiled and headed back for the coffee.

Mick turned his attention back to Samuel. "I'm really thinking that this idea of yours may just work. I know that from the dock to even the store is a bit of a hike, especially for a woman."

In the lobby, Alice saw Ryan walk in the door.

"Hello Ryan, can I do something for you?"

"I was looking for Mr. Dawson."

"Oh, he's in the restaurant with Samuel."

He headed into the restaurant at the same time Mick noticed him.

Mick got up and hugged his best friend. "Ryan, it's been too long."

"I was always here. All you had to do was come on up."

The two men, both all smiles, were clearly were happy to see each other. Mick grabbed another chair for Ryan and had him sit with them.

"Forgive me, Mr. Churchill," Mick said, "but I have not seen this big galoot in over a year."

"No, don't apologize, it's good to see true friends greet each other."

"How's Mary?" Ryan asked Mick. "You said the doctor wouldn't let her travel at this time. Is there some danger to her or the baby?"

"No, but she already lost one last year. She had to take it easy, or she may lose this one."

Ryan felt they could talk about that another time. Right then, they needed to help Samuel with his problem.

Back at the farm, Meghan was sitting in the study, thinking about Christian. *How could he say he wanted to dance with me to see if I danced as well as my sisters? That was just a*

strange request. What if I *didn't* dance at all? Would that make me inferior to my sisters?

Men. They really like to play their silly games. Sitting at home was only making her jittery. Maybe a nice ride with Gypsy would calm her down a bit.

She headed for the stable and saddled up Gypsy. Before long, she was riding across the farmland, her hair blowing in the wind and the sunlight dancing across Gypsy's pure-white mane. She found a sense of peace and freedom when she was on the horse.

Up ahead, Meghan noticed a rider slowly riding ahead of Gypsy. She could clearly see that it was Christian. No mistaking it—no one rode on a horse like that!

She slowed Gypsy's gallop to a trot as she came up beside him.

"Howdy!" she called out.

"Hello."

"Didn't expect to see anyone on the trail at this time of day."

"I was just on my way back from Somerset. There's a very fine doctor there."

"Doctor? You feeling poorly?"

"No. They have a fine doctor there, who has a library of medical books, and he has been kind enough to let me borrow some."

She brought Gypsy to a complete stop.

"You mean to tell me you rode over to Somerset for some medical books?"

"Why, yes. Every week."

"Well Mr. Churchill, you just follow me."

"Where are we going?"

She started to ride ahead of him. "You'll see. I promise, I'll go slowly."

They turned off the main road, and Christian saw the side road that led to the Lochlan farm.

"Hey, we're going to your farm."

"Yep."

"But what—"

"You'll see."

Abby was outside getting the planters ready for the flowers to sprout up. She saw Meghan and Christian approaching the house.

"Hello, Christian," she said. "What brings you out here?"

He looked over at Meghan. "Her!"

"Mama, I'll explain it to you in a bit. Come on, sawbones."

He followed her into the house, past the hall and into the study, where she explained to him, "That whole bookcase is devoted to medical books. The second shelf on the far side is for the anatomy, and these four books are on diseases. You're welcome to borrow them."

He looked around the room. "How did–"

"My grandmother loved to read and collected books on almost everything. She has about six Bibles in here. So make yourself at home and browse."

As she headed toward the door, he called to her, "Miss Lochlan?"

She turned and looked at him. "Look, Christian, don't ya think you could call me by my given name?"

He grinned and shook his head. "You're something else."

"I'm saving you a ride to Somerset each week."

With a smile, she left the room and walked into the kitchen where Abby was getting supper ready.

"I take it you can explain now?" Abby said.

"Christian was riding to Somerset every week, where this doctor seems to have a library of medical books for him to read. Oh, by the way, I forgot to mention that Christian is studying to be a doctor. Anyway, I brought him here. Heck, we have plenty of medical books he can borrow and would save the long trip every week to Somerset."

"That's true. That was very sweet of you, Meghan."

As they were talking, they didn't notice Christian had come to the doorway. He heard what Abby said about her daughter.

"Yes it was," he added.

They both turned and saw the smile on his face as he held a few books in his hands.

"If it's all right with you, I'd like to borrow these."

"Of course it's all right, Christian," Abby said. "Happy that you are getting some good use out of them. Meghan tells me you're studying medicine at college. I think it's wonderful."

"Thank you, Mrs. Lochlan. Oh, you probably know about our grand opening on Saturday. I had asked Meghan to come, and she said she had to see if you and your husband were going."

"Well, Christian, yes. I'm speaking for Mr. Lochlan now. We would love to attend the luncheon with the family."

A big smile came to his face as he looked at Meghan then back to Abby.

"Thank you, ma'am. Well, if you'll excuse me, I have to get back to town. I promised my dad I'd help him with some last-minute details."

"Do stop by anytime. Meghan, will you show Christian out?"

"Yes, ma'am."

When they got to the door, she turned to him. "Well, I guess I'll see you on Saturday."

"I hope to see you before then when I bring back the books."

"That's true."

"Goodbye, Miss Lochlan."

As he rode away, Meghan watched him, thinking about what kind of doctor he would be.

CHAPTER TEN

Ryan came home in the early evening, and Mick was with him. As they walked in the door, Ryan called out to his wife.

"Abby! Where are you?"

Abby came out of the kitchen. When she saw Mick, she ran to him, and he picked her up and gave her a hug.

"Oh, Mick, it's so good to see you!"

Mick put her down and stood back to look at her.

"I can't believe it. Oh, Abby, you're as beautiful as the day I met you."

"Oh, go on with your Irish blarney."

"No blarney, just the truth. You will always be the prettiest girl in Fall River and my sister-in-law to boot. Too bad you're happily married to that smooth-talking Irishman, Ryan Lochlan."

"So tell me, how is Mary? I'm sorry she couldn't be here with you." She took his arm and led him to the living room, where they sat on the sofa.

"She really wanted to come, but the doctor said he didn't advise it. She lost one six months ago. We didn't want to take a chance."

"Oh, the poor girl. Is Holly with her while you're here?"

"Holly is away at school. I expect her to be up for the girls' party. I believe she'll be here with her young gentleman, a boy named Adam Bradford."

His name sounded familiar to Abby, and then it came to her: Adam Bradford was the young man who Meghan had found interesting when she was there.

"I didn't know that Holly had an interest in him, too," Abby said.

Just then, the girls walked in the door.

"Uncle Mick!" they all yelled.

They rushed over to him, and Mick grabbed them in his arms, and they fell on the sofa over him.

"I tell ya," he said, "I don't know which of you is the prettiest, and you are having a birthday soon. I remember the day I first saw you. You were only a few minutes old. Even then, you three were the prettiest girls I ever saw."

"Will you be coming to the party?" Molly asked.

"I'm sorry, precious, but Aunt Mary can't travel, but Holly is coming. She'll be coming with her young gentleman, Adam Bradford."

The look on Meghan's face conveyed that she had seen the devil himself, yet she didn't let on. Abby was the only one who noticed the look.

She got up. "Meghan, would you help me in the kitchen?" She turned to Mick. "You'll excuse me for a moment, won't you?"

"Of course, Abby."

Meghan followed her mother into the kitchen. As soon as she was behind closed doors, she broke down.

"I'm sorry, sweetheart. I had no way to tell you before your uncle sprang it on you."

"It's all right, Mama. I'm used to this sort of thing happening to me. I'm destined to be an old maid."

Abby placed her arms around Meghan. "Don't be silly. You're not going to be an old maid. You'll find the right man one day, and he will be the lucky one to have you. Come on, let's get the table set for supper."

In town at the Churchill House, a few guests were waiting for the train to take them up to Boston. Alice was working in the dining room while Samuel stayed in the main lobby. Christian helped his mother by being in the kitchen, but he wanted to read a book while he was there.

When Alice came into the kitchen, she scolded him. "You shouldn't have that book in here. It might get soiled."

"I'm careful, Mama. Besides, I want to give it back to Mrs. Lochlan tomorrow."

She looked at her son. "Mrs. Lochlan? I think maybe it's another member of the Lochlan family you are interested in."

"Now, Mother, you know I have no time to think of anything like that right now."

"You may not have the time, but there is no way you can stop thinking about it."

She smiled and took the coffee pot into the dining room to serve the patrons. Christian shook his head, but he had to admit his mother was right. He didn't have time for ladies, but his mind did tend to wander toward the Lochlan farm from time to time.

CHAPTER ELEVEN

On the day the Churchills had been waiting and preparing for, the gala grand opening of the Churchill House, the sky was bright and sunny. Thanks to Christian's idea of placing ads about the grand opening in Boston papers, many people were interested in coming and seeing the new hotel.

The Churchills had a busy day in store for them, and Abby offered to help Alice as more guests stopped by for the luncheon.

"I wasn't planning to have you working the kitchen, Abby," Alice said.

"Oh, don't be silly. I'm happy to help out. If we get the girls to handle the dining room, we'll have an easier time to work the kitchen."

"Oh, Abby, I couldn't ask the girls to–"

"Don't be silly. They'll love it. Christian, would you be a dear and get my girls for me?"

"Yes, Mrs. Lochlan."

He headed out the door and toward the front lobby.

Alice turned to Abby and said in a lowered voice, "I have to admit, I think my Christian is sweet on your daughter, Meghan."

"He's a sweet boy, Alice. I noticed that the other day when he was at the house."

Alice smiled. "I'm so glad you're not upset about it. I must admit I wasn't sure how you would feel about it."

"Oh, I think they make a cute couple."

"I'm so glad you feel that way."

Just then, the door opened, and the girls came in with Christian.

"You wanted to see us, Mama?" Meghan asked.

"Yes, I would appreciate it if you and the girls would handle the tables in the dining room while Mrs. Churchill and I keep cooking the food."

"No problem, Mama."

Christian handed each of them an apron.

They put on the aprons and headed out the door to the dining room. Guests filled the room. Only toward the evening did the girls and Abby have time to sit and relax a bit in the kitchen.

Alice came over and said, "Abby, it's wonderful. We have every room filled. I can't thank you all for your help."

Meghan had managed to find a spot out on the back porch to relax. She took off her shoes and just let the air cool her toes. Christian came out and saw her.

"These shoes are not for standing on your feet all day," she said.

"Well, that's a problem. I never liked shoes. I tend to take them off toward the end of the evenings. It just feels so good to have them off."

"You can't do that in the winter."

"Oh, but I have. I've walked in the snow with no shoes on."

She laughed out loud.

He looked at her, amazed. Sometimes she was a young but mature woman, and then in the blink of an eye, she turned into a bundle of childlike energy.

"Have you ever thought what you want in life?" he asked.

"Well, I never gave it much thought. I know you want to be a doctor. And that's a very fine goal in life, but for me... Well, like I said, I never gave it much thought."

"There's got to be something you want to do."

She thought about it for a moment then looked at him again with those gray eyes of hers. "I don't know. There are so many things that I would like to do, but then again I'm not like you. You know what you have planned."

He smiled. "Well, someday you'll find what you want to do."

Abby came to the back door. "Meghan, time to head back home. Put your shoes on."

"Yes, Mama."

Meghan grabbed her shoes and began to put them on when Christian offered to help.

"Let me," he said. "It's hard to get them back on because your feet have swollen."

"It's okay. I'll just leave them off."

"Don't be silly. I'll slip them on and not tie them all the way up."

Alice came out and saw her son on one knee, trying to put a shoe on Meghan.

"My, is that the glass slipper for Cinderella's foot?"

Christian turned a shade pinker. "Oh no, you see, Meghan's feet were hurting her, and well, I told her I could get her shoes back on, but since they were swollen, it's harder to get them on."

Alice just smiled at her son. "Well, when you do get her other shoe on, Abby and Ryan are waiting for her in the front."

After he finished helping her, Meghan took a few steps but then fell and twisted her ankle since her shoes were loose.

Christian picked her up and carried her through the kitchen, dining room, and front lobby and finally to the carriage where her family was waiting for her.

"Meghan, what happened?" Abby asked.

"I started to walk, and I tripped and twisted my ankle."

"Are you sure it's not broken?"

"Well, the good doctor here says it's only twisted."

"She basically just twisted it, Mrs. Lochlan," Christian said. "It's my fault. I really should have let her keep the shoes off. If I had, she wouldn't have fallen."

"Meghan, you needed to keep your shoes on," Abby said.

"I know, Mama, but my feet were so sore, I had to take them off."

Abby sighed and looked at Christian. "Well, I'm glad we have a doctor on call here. Thanks, Christian."

He placed her in the carriage.

"Yes, thanks, Christian," Meghan said.

"My pleasure, Meghan." he turned to her mother. "It would be best if she stayed off that foot for a day and kept it elevated."

"I'll remember that," Abby said.

Ryan said his thanks too and got the horses moving. They headed toward home.

"It's a good thing that Christian was there to help out, wasn't it, dear?" Ryan said, winking at his daughter.

"Oh, I feel the boy has a future in medicine," Abby said.

Meghan had enough of their humor. "I can see this is going to continue until we get home, isn't it?"

"Why Meghan, whatever are you talking about?" Abby said innocently. "We are only discussing how fortunate we were that Christian was there to help you into the carriage."

CHAPTER TWELVE

The next morning, Christian showed up at nine o'clock at the farm to check on Meghan. Annie answered the door.

"Hi," he said, "I came here to check on—"

"Meghan, yes." She smiled and let him in the door.

From the kitchen, Abby called out. "Who is it, Annie?"

"It's Christian, Mama."

Abby came out of the kitchen to greet him. "Good morning, Christian. So good of you to come out and check on Meghan. She's right in the library. You could go right in."

"Thank you, ma'am."

When he came in, Meghan beamed at him. "Hey there, sawbones. See, I'm staying off my foot."

He inspected the ankle. Satisfied that the swelling was going down, he placed the books he'd borrowed back on the shelf.

Meghan was happy he was getting to use the books. Neither the girls nor she showed any interest in medicine.

"So, how are your studies coming along?" she asked.

"Since I don't have to travel to Somerset each week, I'm getting more done, thanks to you. And it helps when the patient listens to the doctor's orders."

Meghan didn't have the heart to tell him she had indeed used her foot to walk around a few times. He was determined to make her stay off it, but anyone who knew her would know one couldn't tell Meghan not do something.

Later that afternoon, Ryan and Mick came galloping up the road. Neither got off his horse.

"Abby! Abby!" Ryan called out.

She rushed out. One look at her husband's face told her something was wrong. "Ryan?"

"Keep the children at home. Do not go into town. We need Christian to come back with us right now."

"Ryan, what's wrong?"

"Influenza. Epidemic."

"Oh my God..."

Christian ran out the door and mounted his horse. Ryan looked into Abby's eyes.

"Promise me you'll stay here. Abby, I want your promise."

"Yes, yes I promise."

"Where's Doc Bailey?" Christian asked Ryan.

"He's in Somerset, and all the roads in and out of Fall River are closed off. There is no train coming to town, either. We're cut off from the outside world."

They headed off to town, and Abby watched them leave, not knowing when she'd see them again.

The men slowed their horses as they entered town. There was pandemonium everywhere. Dixon's store was filled with people trying to buy as much as they could and running back home to lock themselves in their homes.

They rode up to Doc Bailey's office and opened the door. Everyone knew the doctor kept a spare key above the door pane.

"We need all the quinine he has," Christian said. "It's to take the fever down. Mick, I need blankets, lots of them. We'll use the hotel as a hospital. We have to keep the sick isolated from the others. Do you think you could use your influence to have supplies brought up to us by ship? We have to get this under control. They only have to leave them at the dock. We'll carry them up."

"I'll see what I can do," Mick said. "I'll send a wire right now."

"Send a wire to Mary so she doesn't find out from someone else," Ryan said.

"Good idea. I'll meet you all at the hotel."

They make their way to the hotel and found the porch and the main lobby filled with people. Inside, Alice Churchill was holding a young woman who had just fainted in her arms. She saw Christian and called to him.

"She was just talking to me and then said she was feeling dizzy. Before I could get her to the chair, she fainted. She was fine, and now..."

"It's fine, mother. She's just fainted. Ryan, can you help her up to a room? Mother, show him the room."

"Yes. Ryan, please follow me."

Ryan picked the woman up and carried her up the stairs. "I can handle this."

Downstairs, Mick rushed in and addressed Christian. "I sent the wire, but this was waiting for you from Doc." He handed him a folded piece of paper.

Dear Christian,

I'm sorry to do this to you, but you are the only one who can help the townspeople. I can't get back to Fall River. Somerset is quarantined. No one can get in or out. Seems like a fella was passing through. Well, poor soul, he passed on yesterday. I know it's a bit overwhelming, Christian, but I know you can do it.

Doc Bailey

"Well, seems the guy who came through here and gave it to us did the same for Somerset," Christian said.

"Where is this guy?" Ryan asked.

"According to Doc, he passed on yesterday."

"Did you send a wire to Mary?" Ryan asked Mick.

"Yes. I told her I was detained and would be home in a week or two. How are you going to keep Abby at the farm?"

"Oh, she'll stay put."

"Are we talking about the same Abby? The woman you're married to? My sister-in-law?"

"Yes, she promised she'd stay put."

Just then Alice yelled to Christian, "It's your father. Come quickly!"

Christian reached the stairs and saw his father slumped over the banister. "Mother, I'll have Ryan get him upstairs. I want you to give him some quinine. I'll get it up there for you."

"Christian?" She grabbed his arm in fear.

"Mother, go with him. I have others to attend to."

Ryan carried Samuel up the stairs.

All day, Ryan and Mick seemed to be carrying people up the stairs. They had no time to eat. The sick needed to be sponged and dosed with quinine every hour. Christian was too busy attending to them to worry about what could happen to his father.

CHAPTER THIRTEEN

The following morning, Ryan heard the sound of a wagon quickly pulling into town.

Abby drove it right to the front of the hotel. Ryan and Mick rushed outside.

"Something's wrong, Ryan."

They ran over to the wagon and saw both of Ryan's boys in the back.

"They came down with it late last night, but we had to wait till light to get them here," Abby said.

"Mick, get Tom," Ryan said. "I'll get Dan."

Meghan, who was in the back with the boys, got out of the wagon while her mother and sisters rushed inside with the boys.

"Get them upstairs," Christian said to Mick and Ryan.

"I know what you're going to say," Abby said. "I promised Ryan I would stay put, but the boys need medicine, and we're all here to help."

"You can't mean Meghan is here too?"

Meghan had made her way to the front door, but she was limping.

"Yes, Meghan came, and don't you go questioning me, either."

"Fine. Meghan can be in charge of the kitchen." He addressed the young lady. "We need plenty of water for sponge bathing the patients. You can do that without getting in the way." His words were harsh and biting, not at all like the Christian they all knew.

However, Meghan made her way to the kitchen, and that was where she remained.

They all had a long day. When Abby got back to the kitchen, she found her daughter still filling water into pitchers so they had enough to sponge the patients.

"You all right?" Abby asked.

"A little tired, but I'm fine, Mama."

"I'm sorry if Christian was a little hard on you."

"You shouldn't feel bad, Mama. It wasn't your fault. I should have stayed home."

The door suddenly opened, and Ryan helped Alice into the kitchen.

"Abby!" he said.

Abby got a hold of Alice, who sobbed into her arms.

"When?" she mouthed to Ryan.

"Just a few minutes ago. Stay with her, Abby."

"I'm so sorry, Alice," Abby murmured.

"He was so excited the hotel had such a grand opening," Alice said through her tears. "We were going to have your girls' party, and guests that were here last week had already said they would be back. Oh, Abby, what's the use? He's gone!"

"Alice, this is your home. You have Christian, and you have friends."

Alice shook her head. "I've lost my husband. Can you understand that?"

"I do, and I feel for you. But you have to go on."

"Right now, what I need is time to grieve."

Abby stepped away and walked back to Meghan, leaving the woman alone to cry.

A week passed, but many people were recovering thanks to Christian's help. Alice was still coping with her sorrow while Christian had to set his grieving aside, to care for the living.

With the threat of the epidemic almost over, the familiar sound of the train's whistle was eventually heard. The townspeople of Fall River were no longer isolated from the world.

The Lochlan boys were recovering nicely and were able to go home that day. The family climbed into the wagon and said goodbye to Alice.

"Now, you promise if you need anything, you'll call us," Mick said to her. "We're not that far."

"I know. Thank you all. I'll be fine, but do come and visit."

"We will."

During a quiet ride home, Abby turned to Ryan.

"Do you think she'll stay?"

"Hard to say, but when Christian goes back to school, she just might leave. There's not much for her here with Samuel gone."

"I just feel so sorry for her. Besides Christian, Samuel was her life."

"She's a strong woman—stronger than she knows now."

"How do you know, Ryan? Do you honestly believe either of us can know what this woman is feeling right now? I don't think you can or I can."

By the time they got to the house, Abby had stopped talking to Ryan. She got down from the wagon and walked into the house without a word.

"Looks like you've touched a nerve with Abby," Mick said to him.

"She's a bit sensitive right now. She'll be fine."

"I'm not so sure, Ryan."

Time was supposed to heal all wounds. Perhaps it did, but Fall River would take a long time to heal its wounds. So many of its people had passed during the epidemic. So many families were trying to pick up the pieces of their broken lives.

Alice decided to sell the hotel and move back to New York when Christian went back to school. She planned to move near her daughter and maybe even enjoy her grandchildren. To her, the hotel had too many memories, and it was where Samuel had died. The girls' party would be the last function held at the Churchill House.

The guests arrived, and the Lochlan girls greeted them in the lobby. Suddenly, Holly appeared at the door with Adam Bradford on her arm. Meghan and Molly had hoped she wouldn't show, but well, as they'd learned in Washington, Holly needed to be the center of attention.

Meghan felt her heart beating at the sight of Adam. He looked even more handsome than the last time she'd seen him. She found his effect on her strange—she barely even knew the young man. Why did she even care so much that he was with Holly now? It wasn't as if they knew each other that well.

Still, Meghan wanted to escape.

Before she could come up with an excuse, Holly rushed over to the girls. "I'm so glad you still decided to have the party. I mean, with all that's happened, I don't know what I would do if I couldn't come here and celebrate with you three."

"Well, we're glad you came," Meghan said in a flat voice.

"This is Adam Bradford," Holly said. "He is an aide for Congressman Kellogg."

"It's nice to see you again, Mr. Bradford."

Meghan extended her hand to him, meeting his eyes for a split second before looking away.

"My pleasure, Miss Lochlan."

He smiled and took her hand. He held it for a moment then took Molly's and finally Annie's hand as well.

As they make their way to the dining room, Annie looked at her sisters. "Who was that?"

"That, little Annie, was the guy Meghan met in Washington," Molly said. "Seems she left Washington, and Holly moved right in."

"Well, I can see why Meghan was mad. He is handsome."

Molly gave Annie a strange look. Little Annie never used to look at the boys the way Meghan and Molly did. They always assumed she had more important things to think about.

Holly was still showing off Adam. "Aunt Abby, Uncle Ryan, this is Adam Bradford."

"It's a pleasure to meet you, Mrs. Lochlan, Mr. Lochlan," he said.

"The pleasure is all mine, Mr. Bradford," Abby said. "So glad you made it. How is your mother, Holly?"

"Oh, I guess all right. I've been at school. With the baby coming, there isn't much for me to do."

"I thought there would be plenty to do. Someone had to help Mary."

"She has the maid there for that."

Holly turned to Adam. "You know, before we moved to Washington, Mary had to do everything. It's odd how everyone doesn't have a maid."

"Well, my mother doesn't have a maid, and she prefers doing everything herself," he said.

Holly was shocked. "But what about dinners and parties?"

"She's managed it all by herself for the past forty years. I guess she'll keep doing it."

Abby smiled at Adam, and he escorted Holly into the dining room. Then Alice came in, to Abby's surprise.

"Alice, I'm so glad you decided to come," she said.

"Christian thought it would be a good idea."

"I'm glad you listened to him."

Not long after Alice appeared, Christian went into the main lobby, walking up to Meghan and the girls. He smiled at all three of them.

"I just wanted to wish you all a happy birthday." He handed each girl a box.

"I hope you like them, and maybe you'll remember me when you wear them."

Molly opened her box first. "Oh, Christian, this is beautiful. You even had my initials engraved on it."

She held up a beautiful golden heart-shaped locket. Annie was the next to open hers, and like Molly, she had the same locket with her initials. They all looked at Meghan, who still hadn't opened hers.

"Oh, all right."

The lockets were all the same except for the initials.

"I will always think of you when I wear it," Meghan said to him. "It's so sad that you and your mom are leaving."

"With my pa gone and me going off to school in New York, she just didn't want to stay here alone."

Meghan nodded. "I could understand that. But I hope you'll come for a visit every now and then."

"I'd like that. By the way, I wanted to thank you for letting me borrow those medical books. They really kept me up with my studies, and Doc Bailey is sending a letter about how I took care of the town during the epidemic."

"Oh, that's wonderful. You'll be a sawbones yet."

From the other side of the room, Holly noticed Christian talking to the girls. *Who was that handsome fellow?* She slowly moved away from Adam and made her way over to the girls and Christian.

"Hello, I don't believe we've been introduced. I'm Holly Dawson, cousin to the girls."

Christian smiled politely. "Oh, you're Mr. Dawson's daughter. I'm Christian Churchill."

"Churchill? Like the one who owns this hotel?"

"Yes, she's my mother."

"My, it must be exciting to own an establishment as elegant as this one."

Meghan and Molly tried not to roll their eyes. Their cousin was at it again. Holly took Christian's arm and led him out the front door.

"Didn't she come with Adam?" Molly asked Meghan.

Meghan only laughed. "And she left with Christian."

"Is anyone going to tell her he's not rich?" Annie asked.

"Nope." Meghan grinned as she made her way to the dining room and out the side door.

"Poor Christian," Molly remarked.

Annie went to show her mother what Christian had gotten her. "Look, Mama. It even has my initials on it."

"It's very pretty and thoughtful of him."

Meghan headed for the patio since it was the only place she could take her shoes off and no one would see her. When her shoes were off, she dangled her feet in the air.

Left alone inside, Adam had noticed Meghan leave and had an idea where she was heading. He took the nearest door and found her outside on the ledge.

Inside, Abby looked around and then asked Ryan if he had seen Holly.

"She went out the front with Christian."

"Oh!"

"And I just saw Adam head out the side door after Meghan," Ryan added.

"This should be interesting."

"Oh, I'm waiting and watching this one." Ryan grinned.

They continued to smile at the guests out of necessity, but they would sneak a look out at their daughter with the young congressman whenever they got a chance.

Meanwhile on the patio away from the doors, Meghan was still sitting barefoot, her legs still dangling over the wall.

He slowly walked over to her. "Seems like we've been here before," Adam said with an amused smile.

"Here?"

"Well, on a patio—and you with no shoes on."

She smiled at him as she remembered. "Oh that seems so long ago."

"Not that long."

She looked out at the water far below. "Well, maybe not that long."

He noticed his persistence was making her nervous.

She felt an instant attraction between them, yet she didn't know how to deal with it.

Adam could feel the same attraction. He'd felt it the first time he saw her back in Washington, but then she was gone. He thought he would never see her again, but there she was on a patio again—and barefoot. Maybe the universe had decided to give him another chance.

"I really didn't want to upset you."

"Upset me? Whatever for? After all, we had just met that one time in Washington, and I was going back home. That was all there was."

He looked at her. "I would have liked to known more, but when you left, Holly said you wouldn't be interested. She said her mother had offered to keep you in Washington to go to school there but you refused."

"Yes, I refused because I didn't want to end up like all these girls who look down on others and only want to be with the upper class of Washington. I didn't want to be like them."

A smile came to his face.

"Why are you smiling?" she asked.

"Because you're not like all the others. Look at you. Here you are, like the first time I saw you—shoes off, feet dangling in the air. You don't care what anyone thinks about it."

"Well, why should I?"

"Can I tell you something?"

"If you feel you must."

"Well, that evening when I went home, I told my folks I had met a girl who was not like all the others. They didn't believe me. All the girls they've met are girls like Holly—nice girls, but there is no grit, no substance to their being alive."

"But you came with Holly."

"Holly doesn't like to make an entrance alone."

"Oh, I know."

He moved a bit closer and jumped onto the wall beside her.

"So tell me, is it serious with you and this Christian fella?"

"I really don't see whether it's any of your business, Mr. Bradford."

"Oh, but it is, Miss Lochlan. I intend to marry you one day."

She looked at him as if he had lost his mind. "Marry me? And why in the world would I want to marry you?"

"Because, my dearest Meghan, you love me." He leaned over and kissed her.

She pulled back. "I beg your pardon."

He just smiled at her. "Yep, I'm going to marry you in about two years."

"Really, and what makes you think I'd wait for you for two years?"

"Well, for one thing, I won't to be able to support you on an aide's salary. That can't be done. But Congressman Kellogg is retiring in two years and is going to recommend my name to the party to put me up for the seat."

"That still doesn't make you a congressman. You have to win the election." Meghan jumped down off the wall. "I can't be the wife of a congressman. I have no special schooling. I have—"

"You're perfect! You don't have to give me an answer tonight. I will give you one month to think it over. At the end of that one month's time, I will come back for your answer." He gently kissed her again.

"But I—"

"One month, Meghan."

With that, he walked back into the dining room. Meghan was still standing there, not completely comprehending what had just happened.

She had just been proposed to and given a month to answer yes or no.

"That's just crazy."

CHAPTER FOURTEEN

True to his word, one month later, Adam returned to Fall River, and he was not going to take no for an answer.

He was determined to make Meghan see both how much he loved her and how much she loved him even if she didn't think so.

He arrived by train and made his way to the hotel. It was still called the Churchill House. The new owner, Charles Rolle, had liked the name of the hotel enough to keep it. He said it sounded classier than the Rolle House.

Adam had to admit he was right. He walked into the lobby, where Mr. Rolle greeted him.

"Can I help you?" he asked Adam.

"Yes, the name is Bradford. I have a reservation."

Mr. Rolle looked at some cards under the desk. "Yes, I see it right here, Mr. Bradford. Now, if you'll just sign the registry, I'll have someone get your luggage."

"No need. I have my bag here."

"All right, room twelve, top of the stairs to the right. Breakfast from eight to ten, lunch from noon to two, dinner from six to eight."

He headed for the stairs then stopped. "Oh yes, I'd like a hot bath. Can that be arranged?"

"Yes, Mr. Bradford, there is a bath at the end of the hall. I'll have it filled with water and let you know."

"Thank you."

Back at the Lochlan farm, Meghan paced the floor. She had received a letter from Adam, stating he would be there on June 15 for her answer.

She hadn't even told her parents about the proposal yet—mainly because she didn't know how to tell them. She was only eighteen years old.

She heard a horse coming up the road, which could only mean...

She hoped she was wrong, but when she looked out the window, she saw Adam was indeed coming up the road. That would have been a good time to tell her parents what she thought, but it was already too late.

Ryan came to the door when Adam knocked. "Yes?"

"Mr. Lochlan, I'm Adam Bradford. We met a month ago at your daughter's party."

"Yes, I remember you. What can I do for you? If you're looking for Holly, I'm sorry, she's not here."

"No, I'm not looking for Holly."

Abby came to the hall and smiled at Adam. "Do come in, Adam. Seems my husband has forgotten his manners."

"Thank you, ma'am."

"Can I get you something?"

"No, thank you, ma'am."

"So what can we do for you?"

"Well ma'am, I came here to—"

Before he could finish, Meghan came down the stairs. "Mama, Pa, last month, Adam asked me to marry him. He told me I didn't have to give my answer then. He gave me a month to give him my answer."

Ryan looked at his daughter in surprise, then at Adam. "That's very—" He turned to his wife for help.

"Wonderful." Abby was shocked too.

"I think your mother and I will give you two some time on your own. Abby?" He took her hand and led his wife out the kitchen.

Meghan showed Adam into the living room. She sat down on the sofa as Adam stayed standing. He looked at her not with the confidence he had showed the last time he saw her. He was sweating at the brow, and Meghan thought his hands might've been shaking.

"I suppose you want your answer," Meghan said.

"I can wait. Whenever you're ready."

Meghan took a deep breath. "Adam, I am very honored by your proposal, and I really do like you, but I cannot accept your proposal of marriage."

"I don't understand. You care for me, so why won't you want to be my wife?"

"We come from two different worlds. You belong with someone like Holly, a woman who can help you with the political end of your career. I wouldn't know where to start with that. Adam, I'm eighteen years old, not a person you would want to handle the home of someone who is going to be a congressman. I don't know anything about fancy parties and state dinners. What would happen if I totally embarrassed you in front of all your political fiends?"

"Are you finished?"

She nodded.

"Good, now let me tell you where you are wrong. I don't want a Holly in my life, as I stated a month ago to you. As for you not knowing much about politics, I have a wonderful mother who is more than willing to teach you what she had to learn in the last forty years. You see, my mother was not a Washington girl either. When she married Holland Bradford, there was no one to help her fit in. I told her about you, and she wants to meet you and welcome you into the family."

"Your mother wants to meet me?"

"She wants to meet the woman who will one day be the wife of the governor of the state. The fact that will be her son also is another reason why she wants to meet you."

She shook her head, incredulous. "Wife of the governor? I'm not even from the same state!"

He took her hands in his, chuckling a bit. "Meghan, how can make you see I don't want a Holly. I'm not looking for an empty-headed and shallow person only interested in herself. But you, Meghan... You're warm, sincere, and real. I don't know what more I can say to get you to say yes."

She looked into his eyes, and after a few moments that seemed like a lifetime to him, she said, "Ask me again."

He had a gleam in his eyes. He couldn't believe what she had just said. Before she could change her mind, he spoke. "Meghan Lochlan, will you do me the honor of becoming my wife?"

"Yes, yes I will."

She broke out into a huge smile and wrapped her arms around him. He lifted her from the sofa.

Abby and Ryan came into the living room, where they saw both of them glowing with happiness.

"Well, I guess I don't have to ask what your answer was," Abby said. "Welcome to the family, Adam. I knew she would say yes."

"How did you know, Mama?" Meghan asked.

"Oh, let's just say Mother knows certain things, and this was one of them."

Ryan gave his daughter a kiss and offered his hand to Adam. "I know I don't have to tell you to take care of her, so I'll just welcome you into the family."

"Thank you, Mr. Lochlan."

"I think you can call me Ryan. After all, you're part of the family now."

"There's one thing I have to do to make it official." Adam said.

He took a small box from his pocket and opened it. Inside was a ring with a beautiful emerald-cut canary diamond flanked by two smaller rubies surrounded by tiny diamonds. He placed it on Meghan's ring finger.

"This was my great-grandmother's engagement ring. There's a necklace and earrings that go with it. They're part of a set."

Meghan raised her hand up to her eyes. She had never seen anything so beautiful in her life.

"Oh, Mama. Look at how the light bounces off it!" They both started laughing just as the rest of the family came into the living room.

Molly was the first to ask, "What's going on? Hi, Adam." Then she saw the ring on Meghan's

132

finger. "Meghan, you never told me! Never told anyone."

"I didn't know for sure, Molly. It happened so fast. I was sitting on the wall at the party last month, and Adam asked me to marry him."

"I'm glad she said yes, Adam," Annie said.

He smiled at her. "Between you and me, Annie, so am I."

The boys were more concerned with when supper was going to be ready. But then again, engagements were not something a pair of fifteen-year-old boys would be interested in.

Abby shook her head at the boys. "Congratulate Adam. He just got engaged to your sister."

"Gee, Adam, why did you go and do something silly like that?" Tom asked.

Everyone laughed.

Abby realized that though the wedding would be two years away, there were still things that had to be done. The announcement needed to be placed in the paper. Invitations would have to be purchased after a date was set. A formal dinner with both sets of parents would have to be planned.

"Well, I guess I'll get supper ready." Abby said. "Oh, by the way, Adam, you are staying for supper."

"Yes, ma'am."

As everyone headed into the dining room, Meghan stayed in the living room, looking at the light bouncing off her ring. "It really is beautiful. Are you sure you want me to have this?"

"Of course I want you to have it." Adam laughed.

Abby stuck her head out the dining-room doorway. "Are you two going to have something to eat? Come on."

The main topic around the supper table was the engagement. Everyone was in agreement that an announcement of the engagement was in order immediately. There was no mention of a wedding date since it hadn't been discussed; however, the details of how it would happen were a different story.

"Where will the wedding take place?" Molly asked.

"We'll plan a small wedding here on the farm," Adam said. "Would you like that, Meghan? A wedding with just the family and a small dinner party in Pennsylvania so my parents can have their friends meet you."

Meghan looked at her parents. "Do you think that will be all right?"

"It's your wedding," Abby said. "If you like that idea, that's what we'll do."

"Wait a minute, if you win or lose, we are getting married in two years?" Meghan asked Adam.

"Of course we are," he replied.

"Adam, my boy," Ryan said. "Learn early that Meghan is a stubborn woman."

The sound of a horse riding quickly up the road sent Ryan to the front door. As the rider neared, he saw it was Jake Rooney, the telegraph man. He came to a stop and dismounted.

"Ryan, is Mr. Bradford here?"

"Yes, he's having supper with us. Is something wrong?"

"I got a wire for him to come back to Washington as soon as possible."

Adam came to the front door. "Hello, Mr. Rooney. You have a wire for me?"

"Yes, Mr. Bradford, and I have to wait for your answer."

He handed the wire to Adam, and the look on Adam's face showed there was a problem. He looked up at Jake.

"Mr. Rooney, tell Mrs., Kellogg I will be on the next train back to DC. By the way, can you get me a ticket, and when is the next one tonight?"

"Offhand, Mr. Bradford, you would need to go to Boston and take a train from there."

"Fine, make the arrangements for me. I'll be at your office in an hour."

As Jake rode off, Adam handed the wire to Ryan. "I hope you will forgive me for dashing off like this, but I have to get back to Washington."

"I understand, Adam. I'm sorry about the congressman."

"Thank you."

He headed back into the house, followed by Ryan. Everyone in the dining room waited to hear his news.

"I'm sorry I have to cut this short, but I have been called back to DC. Congressman Kellogg has died of a heart attack, and I have to get back to handle some details."

"Oh no," Meghan said. "But where does this leave us?"

"Meghan, we are still getting married, but right now, I have been called to my office and possibly will have to meet with the governor."

"Let's get you to ready to get to Boston," Ryan said.

"I don't want to leave you like this, Meghan."

"Adam, isn't this what I'll have get used to after we marry?"

He looked at her and smiled. He gave her a kiss on the cheek and blew a kiss to Abby. "Take care."

Meghan watched as Adam and her father rode down the road. She realized that would be just the first of many times he would be called away.

Ryan got him to the train station in Boston, and Jake had booked his ticket already. Ryan shook Adam's hand.

"Let us know when you get settled back in DC."

"I will, sir."

CHAPTER FIFTEEN

Three weeks later, Meghan still received no word from Adam, but the newspaper did state that the staff of Congressman Kellogg was making arrangements for his memorial.

Ryan stopped into town for a few things and picked up the mail. He saw a letter from Mick and wondered if it was bad news. He got home and found Abby and the girls on the front porch.

Abby knew from the look on his face that he had some news.

"I got a letter in the mail from Mick," he said. "I don't know what is in it, but I think we should all go inside and read it."

They make their way inside and headed for the living room. The boys, as usual, were out back and had no interest in anything unless food was involved.

Ryan opened the envelope and began to read.

Dear Ryan and Abby,

I wanted to write to tell you that Mary had a baby boy two days ago. We named him Payton after her mamma. Mother and child are doing fine, and Mary can't wait to come and visit you with the new addition to the family. Hope all is well with you.

I don't know if you heard that Congressman Kellogg passed on. He was a fine man. The governor of Pennsylvania is going to appoint in his place his aide, Adam Bradford. He's the young man that Holly was seeing. He escorted her to the girls' party back in May. Well, he's to be acting congressman until the election in November.

I must go. Love to all there.

Mick

Annie smiled as she thought about her aunt. "I'm so glad Aunt Mary has a child of her own.

Mama, do we all have to name our children after members of the family?"

"It's not necessary, Annie. You can choose any name you like."

She seemed content with that answer.

CHAPTER SIXTEEN

In Pennsylvania, Adam wondered if he could get a wire off to Meghan to fill her in on what had been happening. He didn't want her to feel he was too busy to tell her.

He had no idea what she had read or heard from the papers or people, but his constant absence was not how he wanted her to feel their marriage would be, even if he was very busy. Sitting in the study of his parents' home, he was miles away in his thoughts and didn't even hear his mother walk in.

"Adam?"

He looked up at her.

"Is everything all right?"

"I was just wondering how Meghan is handling all this."

She sat down across from him. "Well, let's see, you told me she would be a perfect congresswoman's wife. She has compassion for others. What makes you think she will fall apart at something like this?"

"Mother, she's not like the others, she's..."

"Impulsive, fun, down to earth? Am I doing a good job? She sounds perfect. I can't wait to meet her. Washington needs more wives like her. This country needs more people like her. Matter of fact, I think I'll have an announcement written up in the paper." She got up and kissed him on the forehead. "Don't worry about your Meghan. I have a feeling she'll handle this entire situation well."

"How do you know this, Mother?"

"Because, my sweet son, I did forty years ago."

The following morning, the society section of the newspaper had an interesting bit of news.

Mr. and Mrs. Holland Bradford announce the engagement of their son Adam to Meghan Lochlan of Fall River, Massachusetts. Miss Lochlan is the daughter of Mrs. and Mrs. Ryan

Lochlan and the niece of Mr. Mick Dawson of Washington.

With that post in the paper, every reporter was after Adam for a scoop on who the young lady was and where they met.

Within a week, the press descended on Fall River, and everyone wanted to know all they could about this mystery woman.

With Adam in DC, Meghan was left on her own... until dear cousin Holly came to town.

Holly had everything planned, regarding how to handle the press, and of course, she was always ready for an interview about how they'd grown up. Luckily, Holly didn't come alone. Mick, Mary, and little Payton joined her on the trip, just to keep her in line.

The train arrived early in the afternoon, and two reporters recognized Mick.

"Mr. Dawson, are you here on some business venture for the government?"

"Gentlemen, I'm here with my family for a visit. My wife wanted to see her sister, and I would appreciate you giving us some privacy."

"But Mr. Dawson, your niece—can we get a story on your niece?"

"I have three nieces, and I respect their privacy. I expect you will also."

He made his way down the platform, where a carriage was waiting for him and the family. He helped Mary into the carriage and handed her the baby. Holly was already in the back. Slowly, he made his way out of town toward the farm.

"I just can't believe these reporters," he said. "They're like sharks in a feeding frenzy."

Holly was a bit put out because she would have given the reporters a story on Meghan. "Really, Daddy! After all, some plain nobody from a small town in Massachusetts is engaged to one of Washington's most eligible bachelors, and no one knows anything about her."

Mary gave her a sharp look. "Holly, how can you talk like that about your cousin?"

"Well it's true. She's a nobody."

"Holly Dawson, I will not have you talking about your cousin like that. I want you to treat her with the same respect she and her sisters have given you all these years."

Holly looked down at the floor of the carriage.

"Do you understand what I said?" Mary asked.

"Yes, ma'am."

Mick turned off the main road, and they were on their way up the road to the farm.

Mary looked out of the carriage and waved, a big smile on her face. She couldn't wait to introduce her baby to the family. They rode up to the front of the house, and Abby and Ryan came out the door to greet them.

"Mary! Oh, it's so good to see you," Abby said.

Mick got out of the carriage and handed the baby to Abby as he helped Mary down. Abby moved the blanket to uncover the face of her darling nephew. "Oh, Mary, he's so handsome."

The girls came out and gathered around their mother to see the baby.

"I think he looks like Uncle Mick," Mary said. "Well, the hair at least."

Everyone chuckled as they walked into the house. What they didn't see were the reporters who had followed them from a distance and were interested in a story no matter how they got it.

"Did you see which one was Meghan?" one of them asked.

"I didn't know there were three of them."

"Let's see if we can get a bit closer."

They tiptoed closer to the house, where they hid behind the bushes near the living room. They could hear voices.

"Meghan, I hear congratulations are in order for you."

"Thank you, Aunt Mary."

Molly saw a chance to get Holly a bit more out of sorts. "Show Aunt Mary your ring. It is really beautiful."

Mary raised Meghan's hand higher.

"Oh my, Meghan! That is beautiful. So what are your plans?"

"We haven't set a wedding date as of yet," Meghan said. "We are planning sometime in a year or two from now."

"I see."

The reporters were writing all this down when Mick appeared behind them.

"I thought you two were behind me all the way from town," he said.

"Mr. Dawson, you have to let us get a story," one said. "I mean, everyone wants to know about your niece."

"Since everyone wants to know about her, I think you should come in and meet her. Mind you, if you upset her, I will toss you out on your ears."

The door opened, and Mick pushed in the two reporters. Ryan came into the hall.

"What's going on, Mick?"

"These two men are reporters, and they followed us to get a story on Meghan. Seems they feel they have the right to invade a person's privacy and trespass on the property."

Ryan gave the men a stern look. "I don't know where you people come from, but we are allowed the right to privacy. I have a good mind to wire your paper and make charges against it for trespassing."

"Sir, we are only doing our job. Every reporter is trying to get the story on your daughter and when she is planning to marry Mr. Bradford."

"Don't you think that is going a bit too far? Have we lost all our rights to the press?"

"Sir, she's engaged to a future congressman."

"She's engaged to Adam Bradford, a fine young man. Though he is in the role now, there is still an election that he will have to win to be a congressman. Now, if I let you ask Meghan two questions each, will you leave?"

"Two?"

"Two."

They nodded, and Ryan escorted them into the living room. Meghan looked surprised when the men came into the room.

"Meghan, these men are going to ask you two questions about your engagement to Adam," Ryan said. "Now, they are only allowed two questions, and then they are leaving you alone. Is that clear, gentlemen?"

"Yes, sir," both replied. The men seemed uncomfortable, almost afraid.

"Please do sit down," Abby said.

"Thank you, ma'am," they said.

Meghan gathered enough poise and grace to appear that she did possess the finer qualities of a lady. "I understand that you want to ask me two questions. Since I understand that is impossible for a newspaper man—they really cannot find out the information they need for a good story with just two questions—I purpose to help you on this matter. I will give you a brief story. I believe you in the business call it a 'scoop.' To continue, I will give you the story, and then you will have all you need to know. Does that sound fair to you?"

"Yes, ma'am."

"Good. Well, I will begin by telling you that I met Mr. Bradford at a social event while I was visiting my aunt and uncle in Washington, and then I came back here with my sister Molly. I had not seen him after that until the birthday party our parents gave us this May in Fall River. He came as an escort to my cousin Holly. We talked for a while, and then he left again and came back a month later and asked me to marry him.

"We've made no wedding date as of yet, and with the death of Congressman Kellogg, we are not at this time ready to give a definite date. Now, gentlemen, I do hope that is enough for you to give your editors and that you will give us time to enjoy the company of my aunt and uncle."

They looked at her, surprised at her poise and grace, totally unexpected from an eighteen-year-old.

"Thank you very much, ma'am," one said.

They headed toward the door with Mick and Ryan behind them. Mick made sure they left that time.

"You gave your word," Mick told them. "Make sure you keep it."

They mounted their horses and rode off. Three days later, every newspaper had Meghan's story of the young woman who was engaged to the handsome young congressman.

Adam's mother handed him a copy of the paper when she went to his office.

"Have you read the paper this morning?" she asked.

Adam looked up at her. "No, is there something I should see?"

"The story our little Meghan gave to the press. I tell you, she is a born politician. You should take her on our campaigns."

"What are you talking about, Mother? Meghan doesn't give speeches."

He read the article, which surprised him. She'd handled the story like a pro.

"This is quite good. Matter of fact, this is very good."

His mother smiled. "I told you she would be a good wife for you."

He stood up and kissed her cheek. "Mother, you are right, as always."

CHAPTER SEVENTEEN

The local paper in Fall River wanted an exclusive on Meghan's story, and she was happy to give it to them. After all, she knew those men, and they were like family. They weren't the kind to try to trespass on her family's land to get a story.

Each day, letters came in for Meghan from many women who read her story in the papers and wanted to congratulate her. Dress designers from all over the eastern seaboard wanted to make her wedding gown, with many sending designs or patterns she could look at.

Alice Churchill sent a wire first to congratulate her and second to offer her daughter and son-in-law to make the wedding cake as their gift. The ladies of the Somerset Historical Society invited her to tea and to become a member.

The train pulled in to Fall River that bright afternoon, and the only passenger getting off was Adam Bradford.

Jake Rooney saw him and approached. "Mr. Bradford, is there anything I can get you?"

"Oh hi, Jake. No, I just wanted to stretch my legs before going to the farm."

Luckily, he saw Meghan riding into town on Gypsy. She was as beautiful as he'd remembered, with her long dark hair flowing in the wind.

"Meghan!"

She saw him and smiled, riding over. After she jumped off her horse, she ran into his arms. "Oh, Adam, I've missed you."

"I've missed you too. By the way, I read your story in the newspaper. I must say you impressed me. My mother loved the story. She can't wait to meet you."

"Did she really?"

"She loves you already."

"I have to get a room at the hotel. Come on, walk with me."

"Okay, but you better make sure you come for supper. Mama will be very upset if you don't."

"I wouldn't miss one of your mother's suppers. She's too good a cook. Hey, can you cook like her?"

"Would the marriage be off if I couldn't?"

"No, we'll have your mother move in with us." He laughed and hugged her close.

At the front desk of the hotel, Mr. Rolle greeted them. "So good to see you again, Mr. Bradford. I have your room waiting for you."

"Thank you." He turned to Meghan. "I'll be down in a few minutes, and then we can go to the house."

"All right."

"I can't wait."

Later that night at the farm, Adam was enjoying one of Abby's fresh apple pies.

"I have to admit that they do not know how to make an apple pie in Washington," he said. "I may have seen it all there but not what a real apple pie is supposed to taste like."

Abby smiled. "I'm glad you like it, Adam. But I'm thinking my apple pie isn't the only thing that brought you here to Fall River."

"You're right. Well, the truth of the matter is I wanted to take Meghan back with me and let her meet the people. Oh, they'll love her, and she can stay with my parents. My mother would insist on it."

"And how long would it be for?"

"A week, two at the most. I want the people to see her and love her the way I do."

"I want to go," Meghan said to her mama. "It's the only way I'll know what it is to be the wife of a congressman."

"I promise I wouldn't let anything happen to her," Adam promised Abby.

"I suppose I have to let go someday," Abby said.

The next day, the family was at the station to see Meghan off. The two reporters were there also.

Abby spotted them first and pointed them out to Adam. "Those are the two reporters that Meghan gave the story to. They promised to leave her alone."

"I'll handle them, Abby."

Adam walked over to them. "Hello, boys, I see you're still hanging around Miss Lochlan."

"Well, Mr. Bradford, our bosses said to stay close just in case there was another story."

"I'll give you a story: Miss Lochlan is accompanying me to Pennsylvania. She will be visiting my parents, former judge, Holland T. Bradford, and Eleanor Adams Bradford."

"Can you tell us how long her visit will be?"

"I don't know. As you both know, Miss Lochlan and I are engaged, and though we have no wedding date planned, I trust you will give her some privacy as you would any other person."

"But Congressman Bradford, why is she..."

"Why is she going to meet my mother? Surely you are not questioning why my fiancée would be visiting her future in-laws. My mother has not met her, and she requested this visit. Now, would any of you want to ignore a request from your mother?"

Adam smiled as the reporters shook their heads.

"Gentlemen, if you'll excuse me, we have a train to catch. You're welcome to ride back with us."

"No thank you, Congressman. We'll take the next train."

"As you wish."

He went back to Meghan, who was talking to her parents.

"We should board the train," he told her.

"I know, Adam. Mama, I'll let you know as soon as I get there."

Abby nodded as Ryan placed his arm on her shoulders. They watched Meghan board the train and walk into the car.

"Hold on just a bit more," Ryan said to his wife. "She's going to look out as the train pulls out. Don't let her see you crying."

"Don't worry," Abby said. "She won't."

Meghan looked out the window and waved for the last time as the train pulled out of the station. With Meghan far from her view, Abby slowly let the tears fall down her cheeks.

"There there, Abby. She'll be fine. She's happy. Isn't that what we always wanted our children to be?"

CHAPTER EIGHTEEN

Meghan found the women in Pennsylvania completely different than the girls she had met in Washington. She also found those women accepted her for her honesty, sincerity, and kindness.

As she stood by Adam's side, the people saw what an asset she was, not only to the young congressman but also to the state. Adam Bradford would boast that his winning the election was mainly due to the fact that his fiancée had captured the hearts of the people of Pennsylvania. They had accepted her as one of their own.

As he made his acceptance speech with his parents behind him and Meghan by his side, he smiled at the group of well-wishers.

"I want to thank all of you for your support. A special thank you to my mother, father, and of course Meghan. Now, if you'll excuse me, I'll stop boring you with a long-winded speech. But there is a matter of importance that I must tend to. As you know, two years I ago, I asked Meghan to marry me, and I had promised we would marry after the election. So, with your kind permission, we will go about arranging a small wedding in her hometown."

The crowd cheered as he put his arm around Meghan's waist as they waved to the crowd.

"Oh, when we come back, we will have a reception here for all our friends. That means all of you."

He smiled at the crowd and at Meghan. And so Adam and Meghan were marked at the family farm on November 12, with her family and a few close friends attending as Father Cahill officiated at the wedding.

Alice Churchill did come and, as promised, brought a beautiful wedding cake as her gift. Christian sent his best wishes because, though sorry he couldn't attend, he was taking his turn that weekend to work the emergency room at the hospital.

At Adam's request, the only newspaper allowed to cover the wedding was the hometown paper. They would, in turn, send it to the other papers in Pennsylvania and Washington. The story read as follows:

Meghan Christiane Lochlan, one of the nineteen-year-old triplets of Ryan and Abigail McVinny Lochlan of Fall River, was married today to twenty-five-year-old congressman Adam Holland Bradford, son of the Honorable Holland T. Bradford and Eleanor Adams Bradford of Pennsylvania.

The private ceremony was held at the bride's family home, with only close friends. Attending the ceremony was the bride's uncle, Mr. Mick Dawson, and his family of Washington, DC. A reception followed the ceremony, and the newlyweds were on their way to Pennsylvania, where the Bradfords will host a reception for the young couple.

Meghan was indeed an asset to her husband. Her mother-in-law, who adored her, taught her all she needed to know, and soon, Meghan was having afternoon teas at her home with the wives of other political figures. There wasn't a function she was not invited to.

She even went to the holiday ball at the governor's home. For that Christmas season, Meghan and Adam opened their home to the children of the local orphanage, to have Christmas supper with them, complete with Santa Claus and gifts. Her devotion to the children moved the people, and others soon gave their time and skills to other children in the state.

At the end of Adam's second term as congressman, Meghan was thrilled with the fact that she was expecting. Her sister Molly had had her second child a year before, and Meghan was with child.

She had wanted a child. As matter of fact, she wanted a house full of children. She and Adam had planned on having children since his second term, with no luck until then. They had almost given up hope until she received the welcome news. The child would be due sometime in mid-August.

She told her family when she went home to visit. Abby and Ryan couldn't have been happier. Abby knew how much Meghan had wanted a child, and that was a dream come true.

The dining table had to add another leaf to accommodate the growing family. The glow on Meghan's face was radiant. Her grandmother had always said a woman was the most beautiful when she was with child.

Her brother Daniel's little boy James made himself comfortable sitting on Meghan's lap. James was the fourth child of Daniel, and all he'd had were boys.

"Would you like a girl or a boy?" her mother asked her.

"I'd like a healthy baby," Meghan replied. "I don't care if it's a boy or girl just as long as the baby is healthy."

"Has the doctor told you about slowing down your schedule? I mean, you'll have to rest during the day, you know."

"Well, I told him I would slow down a bit after the holidays. I have a full schedule until February. Besides, Adam has been asked to consider running for lieutenant governor with Governor Horton."

"Meghan, do you realize how grueling that schedule will be for you?" Abby asked.

"Yes, but I also know he needs me there by his side."

"Well, I'm going to tell Adam it just can't be done. You'll be risking the lives of both you and the baby."

"I promise, Mama. I'll be careful."

Once she was back in Pennsylvania, Eleanora Bradford took over the reins, keeping Meghan on a short schedule. She limited her to only two to three appearances a week and made her relax the rest of the time.

Her most recent trip to Fall River was when she was three months from her due date, when she had been hardly able to sit comfortably yet determined to visit home.

Back at home in Pennsylvania, most of her days were spent answering correspondences from Adam's constituents, thanking them for their lovely notes and gifts. Adam was away on speaking tours most of the time, and though Eleanor was there most of the time, at times she felt lonely. She wired her mother to see if Little Annie could come up to be with her for a while.

Annie was on the next train to be with her sister. Little Annie had a calming effect on Meghan, and with her there, Meghan felt the comfort of home. They would spend afternoons walking—and sitting down frequently—but walking still and, of course, reading the latest books.

The week before Meghan's due date, Abby and Ryan had come up to be with her. Adam was campaigning. After all, the baby still had a week to go, but as everyone knows, babies don't always follow a schedule.

Right in the middle of supper, Meghan thought she was having pains from sitting too long. She got up and doubled over in pain, holding on to the table to sit back down.

"Ladies, I think it's time," she said to Eleanor and her mom.

"Oh my," Eleanor said.

Abby got up and gently helped Meghan up. Annie helped Abby get Meghan into the bedroom.

"Let's get her in bed and prop her up so she's comfortable."

Once in the bedroom, Abby looked for Ryan around the house.

"I need you to get to Adam and tell him he's got to come home," she said when she found him. "Does anyone know where the doctor is?"

Eleanor came in. "He's with Adam and my husband, at the debate."

"Ryan, hurry," said Abby.

Meghan cried out in pain.

Abby rushed into the bedroom to help Meghan. "Annie, I need you to boil water, and we'll need plenty of clean towels."

"We're going to have to deliver this baby if the doctor doesn't get here soon," Eleanor said.

"I've never done—"

"Not to worry, I was a nurse before I married Mr. Bradford."

Abby was relieved when the woman jumped in to take over. It was a good thing since it looked as though Meghan was not going to have an easy time of it.

"Now, Meghan," Eleanor said, "I'm going to help you along since the doctor is taking his time getting here. I don't want you to be worried, so I'm letting you know I was a nurse before I was the judge's wife. I'll tell you how I met the judge. I was working in the hospital, and this handsome man came into the emergency room with a bad gash on his leg. Seemed he and some friends were trying to see who could jump over a barbed-wire fence."

Meghan cried out in pain.

"Well, you can guess who didn't make it over the fence. It was a nasty gash too. Well... okay, Meghan, now you do what I tell you, and we'll have an easy time of this. Take a deep breath and push!"

Annie gave Meghan her hand to hold as she pushed. Abby was trying to prop Meghan up so she was in a half-squatting position. Eleanor saw the baby but not enough yet. Meghan cried out with another contraction.

"Okay, Meghan! Breathe again and push!"

Annie's hand felt as though it would break because of how hard Meghan was squeezing.

Ryan found Adam at a hall a good eight blocks from the house, still in the middle of a debate. He saw Ryan and immediately realized the urgency of his visit. Ryan rushed up to the front of the stage and gave the moderator a note stating that Meghan was in labor and about to give birth. The moderator gave the note to Adam, who stopped his rebuttal speech and looked at the audience.

"I must apologize, but I can't go on tonight. My father-in-law over there has informed me that my wife is in labor at this very moment, and I should be there with her. I hope you don't mind me leaving at the middle of this, but–"

Someone from the audience yelled, "Go take care of our Meghan, and let us know if it's a boy or a girl!"

Adam smiled from ear to ear and headed out the door followed by Ryan, his father, and the good doctor.

Back at the house, Eleanor encouraged Meghan to go on. "One last push, and it's all over. Push!"

With a loud cry, Meghan gave the push all she had. The cry of a newborn filled the room just as Adam and the other men came in through the front door.

"Well, son, sounds like you're a father," said the doctor.

"I should go in and make an appearance," Adam said, rushing up the stairs.

He ran into Annie, who was coming out the door. She found the men looking at her expectantly and couldn't understand why until realization hit her.

"Oh, sorry! It's a boy. Meghan's resting right now. She's had quite a lot of activity."

"Did you and Meghan discuss a name for this new Bradford?" the doctor asked Adam.

"We had thought of a lot of names, and Meghan had a great uncle that was special to her mom. She wanted to give it to the boy as a middle name."

"That's a great idea," Ryan said.

"You still haven't told us the first and middle names," Annie said.

"Ah yes, he will be named Jason Gideon Bradford."

Eleanor came out, holding the new Bradford for all to see. "Jason, meet your father and grandfathers."

Adam held his precious newborn son in his arms. "Hi there."

He could've sworn he saw a hint of a smile on the baby's lips.

"By the way, how did the debate go, Adam?" Eleanor asked.

"The debate... Oh, Lord, I left in the middle of my rebuttal."

"Ryan," Adam's father said, "care to come with me while I tell the people the good news?"

"Don't mind if I do, Holland."

As Abby and Annie helped Eleanor with young Master Jason, Meghan continued to sleep.

Adam took a peek into the room at his lovely wife.

"She's had a workout," Eleanor said softly. "She needs her rest."

"She's healthy, isn't she?" Adam turned to her mother.

"The good doctor says she's young, strong, and healthy and should be up and about in no time at all."

Adam stood at a podium, about to take the oath of office as the Lieutenant Governor of the commonwealth of Pennsylvania.

Young Jason sat on his Aunt Annie's lap. Raven-haired, with bright blue eyes, he was likely to break a lot of hearts when he got older.

The pride in Meghan's eyes was obvious to everyone around her as she watched her husband repeat the words of the oath as he was sworn in by his father, the Honorable Holland T. Bradford.

She knew Adam could be anything he wanted. Whether he would be a governor next or a senator, a cabinet member, vice president, or even the president of the United States— those were all possibilities that lay before the young man.

After all, at twenty-five, he was just a baby in the political circles. He had so much time to accomplish all that he wanted, but no matter what position he held, Meghan knew one thing: she was happy and proud to be his wife and the mother of his child.

ABOUT THE AUTHOR

Chloe Emile writes sweet, clean romance, whether it's contemporary or historical. She can usually be found working on her next novel, eating takeout with her husband, or watching rom-coms.

www. ChloeEmile.com

Chloe Emile

www.ingramcontent.com/pod-product-compliance
Lightning Source LLC
Chambersburg PA
CBHW032211170626
46808CB00006B/2429